ROCKAWAY

TARA ISON
ROCKAWAY

A NOVEL

SOFT SKULL PRESS
AN IMPRINT OF COUNTERPOINT

Rockaway
Copyright © Tara Ison

Library of Congress Cataloging-in-Publication Data

Ison, Tara.
 Rockaway : a novel / Tara Ison.
   pages cm
 ISBN 978-1-59376-516-3 (alk. paper)
 1. Artists--Fiction. 2. Inspiration--Fiction. 3. Revelation in art--Fiction.
 4. Aging parents--Care--Fiction. 5. Domestic fiction. I. Title.

PS3559.S66R63 2013
813'.54--dc23

                    2013002746

Cover design by Debbie Berne
Interior design by Tabitha Lahr

Printed in the United States of America

SOFT SKULL PRESS
An imprint of COUNTERPOINT
1919 Fifth Street
Berkeley, CA 94710
www.softskull.com

Distributed by Publishers Group West

10 9 8 7 6 5 4 3 2 1

to Michelle

ROCKAWAY

SHELLS

THIS IS WHAT I'll paint, she decides: shells.

She is staying in a beach house at the last edge of asphalt before sand, a home that belongs to her best friend's grandmother, who is away recovering from hip replacement surgery. She is here, emphatically, to paint. Back home in San Diego, a gallery owner, impressed by Sarah's art store display canvases daubed with rich Old Holland oils, had proposed an exhibit. If there were some *interesting, recent* work, perhaps. Paintings that expressed and defined who Sarah is, now. This was an important opportunity, she realized, something worthy of focus. But can't you paint here?, her parents had asked. There are too many distractions here, friends, work, family, she'd replied, hitting the *fam* hard, like in *fam*ine.

You'll be fine without me, she told them. I need to do this. I need to get away.

She called her best friend in Connecticut, who'd married a millionaire and now had a country estate where they planted a garden for the pleasure of growing their own fennel and arugula. They raised sheep to knit their own lumpy, organic sweaters from. The cost of feeding and shearing the three sheep, and having their wool carded, came to over a thousand dollars a sweater. Sarah tried not to envy her friend these sweaters, but it was hard. Instead, she called the friend to request a haven.

Emily, about to have her third child by water birth, told her with kindness it wasn't a good time right now, and then generously offered her Nana Pearl's house in Rockaway, New York. Right on the beach, Emily said, it would feel like home. It would be empty for three or four months during the convalescence, except for Bernadette and Avery, the caretaker couple who lived in a studio guesthouse. She could stay there the entire summer. No one would bother her. The perfect retreat. And,

This'll be really great for you, Sarah, Emily enthused into the phone. I'm so happy you're doing this, finally.

Sarah quit her longtime default job managing the upscale art supply store in La Jolla, California, a blandly beautiful seaside town outside of San Diego where she had grown up. For years she'd shaved off ten percent of her paycheck and put it aside the way Mormons do to secure the earthly or heavenly future; she figured she'd saved just enough money to live, for a while. She gave notice on the beige, formica-and-asbestos, meant-to-be-temporary apartment she'd lived in since coming home from college, garage sale'd most of her kitchenware and furniture to San Diego State freshmen, and jammed the rest of her belongings, boxed-up and blanketed, into an 8' by 7' by 5' storage vault she rented for thirty-five dollars a month. She broke up with her shrugging, default boyfriend, David. She packed up palettes and fresh brushes and fat, unpunctured tubes of paint, solvents, primers, and siccative oils, set her email to an emphatic auto-reply (*I am currently offline and unreachable, away on a painting retreat!*), and instructed her parents not to call.

Of course we understand, they said, of *course* we'll be fine, don't be silly, this will be so wonderful for you, go, go!

The Rockaway house—one of the oldest in the neighborhood, she remembers Emily telling her, 1902 or '03—was surprisingly huge, dark gray stucco and fancy white trim, an awkward blend, she thought, of late-Victorian gothic and Cape Cod seashore glamour. The house, set off from the sea and sand by a low brick wall encircling the property, was at the dead end of a small flat street off Rockaway Beach Boulevard, at the western peninsula tip of Long Island, ten minutes of highway and one bridge across Jamaica Bay from Brooklyn. The house's longest stretch on the second floor spanned seven bedrooms and three bathrooms linked without hallways, all with ceiling-high windows facing the gray-green Atlantic and full of wave crash and sea-tanged air. Her friend Emily's mother Leah, plus Nana Pearl's five other children, had grown up here; the house was peopled with photographs of these children, their children, and their children, including a recent shot of Emily with pregnant stomach and beatific smile, her husband and their two exquisite kids in their lumpy homeknit crewnecks. Dozens of eyes gazed on as Avery, the husband of the caretaker couple, guided Sarah upstairs, past walls collaged with grinny family photos.

"And this is Aaron, and Michael, Leah, and Rose," he said, pointing. "And this is Rose's daughter Susan, and this is Fran's son and his girlfriend, and—"

"I know all these people," Sarah said politely. She and Emily had been best friends since third grade.

"Ah, you are knowing Emily? This is Emily, with her husband and the children . . . "

They eventually arrived at the largest corner upstairs room, an oblong with huge picture windows on two sides framing the Atlantic Ocean like seascapes, gritty hardwood floors, threadbare rugs, and a queen-sized bed with a white iron headboard and flowered chenille spread. Waiting for Sarah was a large box shiny with packing tape, crammed full with the stretched and framed blank canvases she'd UPS'd ahead.

"This is a good room for you, yes?" Avery said in a booming, Sri Lankan lilt. He was a squat barrel-type man, ochre, tattooed, his bald head rooted solidly to his shoulders. "This is Pearl's room. So much sunshine. You can be looking out. It is good for you and your painting."

"It's great. Really, thank you," Sarah said. She swung open one of the picture windows, breathed in the turquoise light, the inviting sweep of beach, the steady seashell hum. She couldn't remember when she last went swimming in the ocean, at home, but this ocean looked richer than the Pacific, more promising, as if undersea jewels and magical, tentacle'd creatures awaited. She graciously tried to tug her bags from him, which he had insisted on carrying for her.

"And here are many rags for you, for the painting. But I am thinking, you will not be lonely here?" He looked concerned.

"Oh, no. I'm here to work. I'm getting ready for an exhibition." She smiled gaily at him, studied the room—the easel, that'll go there, by that window, maybe clear off that nightstand, yes—and began to unpack her palette knives from the small wooden case she'd clutched to her side. I have an entire summer, she thought. Today is May 2nd. No, the 3rd. May 3rd, 2001. I have three months, maybe four. She envisioned filling her blank canvases with color, form, expression, and bringing them forth into the world, the rich smells of linseed oil and turpentine mingling with the ocean salt, infusing the house with her artistry, her presence. "I'm here for the working," she said, in response to his skeptical face. "The being alone is good. It's perfect. It's what I'm wanting." She hoped the gerunds would make it easier for him to understand.

IN HER FIRST moments on the empty beach—A walk first thing will clear your head, she tells herself, freshen and focus your vision, maybe you'll even go for a swim in that promising sea—she spots a clamshell larger than she's ever seen, sticking up from the sand like a highway-divider flap. She brushes it free of grit and plans to hold onto it as a keepsake of this time, until she realizes the entire beach is mosaicked with these huge clamshells, like expensive, themed floor tiling. She switches her allegiance to oyster shells, which, though plentiful, are smaller and harder to spot in the sand. Every day after her morning toast and coffee, then again in the late afternoon before tea and fruit, she makes a ritual of striding the sand to gather one or two oyster shells hued in grays, only the rare, perfect, unbroken ones. They look like little spoons, she thinks. If you were trapped on a desert island, you could collect oyster shells to make yourself spoons. She pictures herself shipwrecked, blissfully, eternally alone, living on seafood and shredded coconut, painting with fresh-squeezed squid ink and wild berry juices. She brings the shells up to her room—pausing to rinse them, and her bare feet, free of sand with the hose Avery leaves on the front porch—and lays them out carefully on the dresser top she's cleared of Nana's prolific family photos; as the days pass it looks like dinner service for four, then six, then eight, then twelve, awaiting a houseful of convivial guests and a course of soup. She shreds open her UPS box, carefully props her canvases against the walls of her room, arranged so their creamy faces can gaze expectantly upon her.

She remembers an old prison movie from TV, where the warden warns an incoming inmate in a voice lethal with courtesy: *Your time here can be hard, or your time here can be soft. It's all up to you.*

Exactly, she thinks. She feels buoyant, untethered, full of faith.

"AH, YOU ARE finding a shell!" says Avery's wife Bernadette. She has sooty hair in a thick spine of braid down her
back, a wizened apple-doll face. Sarah has placed an albescent clamshell near the kitchen sink as a spongeholder, and
Bernadette nods acceptingly at this new addition to the
household. She and Avery comment on her every action
when she's in the kitchen—Ah, you are cooking now?—
making her self-conscious. She had not realized they would
all be sharing the kitchen, that she would feel so observed.
They are intrigued by her way of roasting broccoli, how she
disassembles an artichoke. So much work, grinding the
coffee beans every morning! Do you not like spicy food?
they query in thunderous voices, making her feel bland and
defensive. They are the type of intrusive people she always
winds up being unavoidably rude to, and then feeling guilty
about. She begins taking her meals on plates up to her stu-
dio/bedroom, ostensibly to eat while she paints. When they
cook, after she's left the kitchen, their shouted, mingled lilts
to each other and the smells of curry and cardamom waft.

During beach walks her head pulses with the *(interesting, recent)* art she will make. Images flash in bold, flat-
bristled strokes; shapes and colors snap like flags. The new
work will offer insight. Will communicate and express her
vision. But when she returns to her easel overlooking the
sea, the visions split off to pixels, scattered as broken bits of
shell in the sand. Her blank canvases stare at her, wide-eyed

and waiting. The pulses creep into faint throbs at the back of her head.

Relax, Sarah, she tells herself. You haven't done this in a while, is all. You're not used to having this kind of time and focus and space. You're still acclimating. Don't overworry it.

She starts carrying a sketchpad with her on beach walks, one of the many bought for this sojourn, all hard-backed like bestsellers. She dutifully strolls back and forth along the shoreline, admiring the expansive and eclectic beachfront houses—Cape Cod, Queen Anne, Art Moderne—sits on a baby dune of sand, cracks the pad open to thick, blanched pages. But then, sitting and clutching a stick of pricey high-grade charcoal, she sees nothing. Her hand wavers over the page as if palsied. The sunlight hurts her eyes, blanks out her brain. The breeze threatens her with grit. It is oddly chilly here, for summer. She retreats into the house with the sheet of paper ruined, crisped from sun and sticky with salt, all for nothing.

The tap water here runs out cloudy; when she fills a glass she must pause for the swirl of opaque minerals and molecules to settle. The glass clears from the bottom up, fizzing slightly, while she jiggles a foot, holding the slippery glass carefully, waiting.

You have to remember, she thinks: Rituals take time. They are invisible in the happening, we don't see them until they have become.

She decides not to shower or wash her hair until she has completed one perfect painting.

———

BERNADETTE AND AVERY recycle; there is a box for used cardboard and paper, one for glass, one for plastics, one for metals. One bag holds flattened aluminum foil, veined from use. They pillage the kitchen trashcan, looking for anything that has slipped through the system. Sarah is annoyed at their quizzical examination and redistribution of her wrappings and peelings. She takes to packing up her garbage in her backpack—the empty bottles, the hair combings, the used dental floss and tampons, the ruined sketch pages—to drop privately in a public Dumpster when she goes into town, and listens to the explosive, packaged clink of breaking glass with satisfaction. She has walked to and from the nearby specialty deli shop twice, carrying her milk and produce, overpriced German beer and French pinot noir, an expensive bag of coffee beans, the splurge on ultra-dark European chocolate, but eventually Avery insists on the need for a bicycle—the nearest grocery store is thirty blocks away, down the long strip of Rockaway Beach Boulevard that spines the length of the peninsula. He pulls from the shadowy garage a girl's rusting bike, left by one of Nana's children or grandchildren, wheels it down the driveway. He affixes a pink wicker basket, fusses happily with bolts and air pressure and alignment. She watches, nervous, eyeing the back-and-forth traffic down on the boulevard, tucking the hems of her long cotton pants into her socks; she has not ridden a bicycle in years, is embarrassed at her awkwardness in mounting and her little yelps of fear as she test-pedals around their quiet dead-end street. A subtle memory teases: her father teaching her to ride a bike, she remembers, sees him running alongside, patient and panting in warm summer sun, holding the high looped sissy bar steady so she won't fall, then letting go, watching and cheering her on. She remembers breeze, the sense of freedom and flight, then relives the sudden wobble, the panic, the skid, an abrupt falling, the hot pain of skinned knees leaking small grids of blood. She remembers his feet, adult rubber soles running to her, his strong adult hands and comfort murmurs, the soothing sting of antiseptic. The reassuring plasticky smell of a Band-Aid. *Okay, so you'll be okay, Sarah? Then let's get you back on that bike!* Climbing back on that bicycle, yes, steadied for her by his hand and encouraging smile. She remembers her newly emboldened pedaling. She smiles at the memory. Faint as ghosts now, all those babyhood scars.

She shakes her head, and clutches harder at the handlebars. Avery, clasping a wrench, nods approvingly and points her toward civilization. She turns onto Rockaway Beach

Boulevard, gasping a little at every jolting chink in the road, accompanied by the tinny and self-generated *pling pling* of the bicycle's bell. Cars pass her by like benevolent sharks, and ten or twelve blocks along finally she relaxes enough to unhunch her shoulders and look around.

It's a time-warped, patchwork little neighborhood, a jumbled mix of blue-collar row houses with tiny, well-tended front-lawn patches of grass, larger Arts and Crafts bungalows with encircling porches and wicker furniture, modest mid-century ranch-style homes, and the odd glass brick-and-concrete Postmodern effort, all of it entirely unlike the faux-Mediterranean, gated-community sprawl of La Jolla. She remembers Emily's history of Rockaway, the once-upon-a-time playground of elite New Yorkers looking to escape the city heat and summer at the beach; now there are large, shabby-looking buildings in the distance—housing developments? she wonders, warehouses, abandoned factories?—bruising Brooklyn accents—although yes, she remembers, Rockaway is technically part of Queens—kids yelling in Spanish and the constant *thwunk* of basketballs somewhere on cracked schoolyard macadam. She passes so many synagogues, yeshivas, and Catholic churches she begins to wonder if she is pedaling in circles, until she spots the commercial district up ahead, at the intersection of the boulevard and Beach 116th Street. There is a liquor store, a Baskin-Robbins, and a lingering Blockbuster, a chain grocery store she has never heard of, two hardware stores, a Chinese restaurant, a CPA, the dime store where Avery works part-time, a Buy the Beach Realty, and a Pickles and Pies Delicatessen—Egg & Roll, $2.39. There is the subway station for the A train that sweeps down through Manhattan for its long stretch across Brooklyn and Queens, tunnels beneath Jamaica Bay, and emerges onto the Rockaway peninsula to spit out weary passengers. There is also a ladies' apparel place, which Sarah at first mistakes for a vintage clothing shop, offering the print dresses and quilted housecoats her grandmother used to wear, the window mannequin wearing a sagging nylon brassiere and cut off at the waist. She buys turpentine at one of the hardware stores. She buys a knish.

In a junk shop she finds a thick book: *A Collector's Guide to Seashells of the World*, which she buys with the notion of identifying some of those scattered shells she's seen; her walks on the beach, now, will be purposeful, will be research. She pedals home on the rickety *pling*ing bicycle, her thighs burning. The pretty cover photo of a mollusk trembles in the wicker basket—This is what I'll paint, she thinks, pleased: shells—and she rides over the road cracks carefully; there is a new half-gallon of merlot in her backpack, and she worries that if she falls the bottle will shatter and a shard will puncture her, nick her spine or pierce a lung.

When she gets the book home, however, she finds the written part of *A Collector's Guide to Seashells of the World* laborious, obsessed with classification and boggy Latin words; *Mollusca-Gastropodae-Mesogastopoda-Cypraeidae-Cyprae-Tigris* bears no relation at all to the glistening tiger stripes, the whorls, the fierce horny spines, the sinuous geometries, the corallines and saffrons and ceruleans of the shells in the book's generous color plates. She normally doesn't like photographs, hears the impassioned rant of an old art professor: *A photograph is a dead image of a dead thing! It's painting, a painting, that creates and gives life!* But she has to admit the color photos outshine the prosaic, monochromatic shells she's actually found on the beach. Perhaps the photos will serve as a prompt, she theorizes. The juxtaposition of glossy dead thing with imperfect real specimen. And so she spends an hour or so each morning leafing through the book over her fresh-ground, cooling coffee, idly admiring the rainbow color rays of *gaudy asaphis* clams and the fluted projecting scales of giant clams, also known as crypt-dwellers.

———

THERE ARE THREE different kinds of sand to walk on, she discovers. On the other side of the low brick wall that marks Nana's property, farthest from the water, the sand is dry and siftable and pale as snow, the warmest to bare feet but the most dangerous with its buried broken things, sharp fragments of plastic and glass, bits of abandoned toys.

The next section is slightly damp, toughened and stiff from the last lunar swell of surf, and the most obstacled with shells, seaweed, ragged seagull feathers, twisted limbs of wood. This sand almost carries her weight without breaking the surface.

Then the wet, darkest sand, briefly and constantly re-soaked with each slow roll and break of a wave. When she steps here she craters the sand for a mere second before her foot trace is swirled away. She lingers, slushing her feet back and forth in a few inches of cold briny water, liking how she seems to disappear with each step.

When she heads back to the warm sand up by Nana's, she notices a man in shorts studying the house, thick-tor-soed but with long and shapely legs like a cocktail waitress; he exits the beach onto the small street and disappears from view. Another man, she notices, is sitting placidly on Nana's wall, wearing sunglasses, a dark sweatsuit, and black knit cap, curly hair fringe flapping in the breeze. He is unshaven, bum-like. She is annoyed at their presence; it is disruptive.

The early-May beach has been blessedly empty, the ocean and bright air still too chilly for bathers, not even a lifeguard on duty yet atop the high rickety chair facing the sea, and she's used to having the span of shore all to herself. She is looking forward to swimming, soon; maybe she'll begin each day with a brisk, invigorating ocean swim. She sits several yards away from the bum-like man and leans her back against the wall proprietarily, prepared to sketch. After a moment she pulls aside her long cotton skirt and exposes her legs, hoping to maybe get some color in the weak sun. She inspects her pale and stubbled calves and thighs, so dry these days, her skin, something she should take better care of. Maybe get some Vitamin E oil, they say that works well, diminishes the marks of time, of old scars. She rubs at her thigh, remembers glowing a perfect unblemished peach, her apricot child skin, her tender, once-upon-a-time skin. She drifts her fingers through the sand, sifts free a shard of glass, bottle-green, like old ginger ale bottles, she thinks, apricot and green, the vibrant colors of those little-girl summer beach days. The ritual stop at 7-11 to buy Coppertone and bruised blushing apricots and those emerald bottles of ginger ale to pack with crushed ice in the cooler. At the La Jolla Shores they'd choose the most isolated spot, stab an umbrella deep, spread beach towels extravagantly.

She always swam off by herself, she remembers, leaving her parents and baby brother with their radio and magazines and baby-boy toys. She remembers the happy stumbling sandy run, the blithe, flapping free dive into the sea, the euphoria of swimming deep. The brief fear as the solid world dropped away beneath her, then surfacing, feeling and realizing the effortless float, the joy of floating free, arms outstretched to greet the next wave. And after each wave came, flipped and roiled her underwater like a scrap of paper and dragged her back to where the ocean broke down and thinned, she'd scramble up from the seaweed and sand crabs, cough, and look for them, her parents, eyes burning and searching and the start of another fear, of panic, but there, always, every single time, there they are. Her parents, watching for her.

Her father waves, proud and affirming, her mother applauds overhead, making it okay to swim back out all over again alone to meet and conquer the next swelling, frothing wave. When she has enough brine in her throat she staggers back, to her mother's fresh palmful of coconutty Coppertone, a popped-open bottle of that cold ginger ale, a piece of bruised fruit sweating ice, sweet things to cancel the salt and soothe. A brisk rub with a sun-hot towel, their admiration and cheers for a discovered shell, a perfect seaweed fan, the tiny sand crab she's carried home in her cupped palms, the painstaking drawing she's made—*Mommy, Daddy, come see, come look!*—of a perfect seahorse or mermaid or happy family of fish in the damp sand.

You should give them a call, she thinks, blinking. Really, you should call, see how they're doing, if they need anything. You should check in with them, they've been so understanding and supportive and not bothering you. She studies the piece of glass, so careless of people, really, to bring glass things to the beach, just breakage waiting to happen and then all those glinty bits hidden in sand, lying in wait for soft feet and fingers and toes . . .

"Hey!"

She is startled, looks up. She spots the man in shorts exiting the front gate of Nana's house, approaching. She flips her skirt back down again.

"Hello?" she inquires.

"You Sarah?" he asks loudly.

"Who are you?"

"You know Susan?" Susan is her friend Emily's first cousin.

"Uh, yeah."

"I'm her dad's brother. You know Rose, right?"

Rose, Sarah knows, is Susan's mother, her friend Emily's aunt. One of Nana Pearl's four daughters. Rose was divorced from Susan's father Bruce when Susan was seven. Sarah knows the twining course of Emily's complicated family history as well as she knows her uncomplicated own, all those Emily-family gatherings she's attended, the holidays, weddings, Bar Mitzvahs, graduation parties, the being invited along to birthday celebrations in Catalina, their clannish ski trips to Vail.

"Uh huh," she says.

"Yeah, I still talk to her a lot, you know, she and Bruce're still pretty good friends. Heard you were here. Thought we'd come by, say hello." He gestures behind her, to include in his *we* the man still sitting on the wall, who is ignoring them, studying the sea.

"Oh. Hello."

"So, you're what, on vacation?"

"No, I'm here to paint." She closes her sketchbook, picks up her sandals, rises; she will have to pass right by him to get to the house. She puts the piece of glass in her pocket, to dispose of properly in Bernadette's kitchen recycling.

"Oh, hey, you're an artist?"

"Well," she says.

"Great. Hey, Marty," he yells, "we got an artist here!" The man on the wall finally looks over at them, and now does. He swings his sweatsuited legs over to their side, like a concession.

"So, what, you want to go for a walk with us?"

"I was just about to get back to work," she says, approaching them. "I'm here for painting. I'm getting ready for an exhibition." *Mommy, Daddy, come see, come look!* she remembers.

"Oh, come on, take a break. Come for a walk with us. Marty," the man yells, "come get her to go for a walk with us."

"What's your name?" she asks.

"I'm Julius. Bruce's brother Julius. This is my friend, Marty. We grew up together. Marty still lives here, just a few blocks over. Tell her, Marty."

Marty points in the direction of a few blocks over.

"Yeah, Marty's an artist, too. Musician." Julius tells her the name of a band that sounds slightly familiar, like a group mentioned in a *Sounds of the Sixties* album commercial. "Big glory days. Ever hear of them?"

"Maybe."

"So, there, see? Come on, come for a walk with us." He reaches, puts his hand on her arm, and she is glad to be wearing a long-sleeved blouse. He has skin either an enhanced or natural nut brown, and a ruby red, pouty lower lip.

"I don't know . . . "

Marty strolls over. He takes off his sunglasses, looks at her inscrutably, and nods. Closer up he looks like a pleasant-faced but aging actor in a going-psychotic role.

This is how women's cut-up bodies wind up washing ashore, she thinks. This is how it starts.

———

AS THEY WALK along the shoreline, on the damp, toughened strip of sand, Julius tells of his youthful escapades. A buddy once invited him to a concert in New York and he found himself on a helicopter to Woodstock, where, Jimi Hendrix's manager having not shown up, Julius walked around for the weekend wearing Jimi Hendrix's manager's security badge and doing drugs with John Sebastian. Another time he wound up schlepping a suitcase of opium across Europe, and getting busted in Israel. They kept him in jail for six months, finally letting him go the first night of Hanukkah, he thinks, because he's a Jew. Not much of a Jew, hafta say, Julius says with a laugh. Now, Marty, *that's* a Jew, a real Jew. He's started keeping kosher, the whole bit. Getting conservative on me these days.

Marty bobs his head in good-humored acknowledgment.

"You Jewish?" Julius asks her.

"Yes. But not much of one, either," she says.

Now Julius is a stockbroker in Manhattan. He still keeps in touch, though; he manages a Cuban musician and twice a month flies to Havana for club dates and banana daiquiris at one of Hemingway's favorite bars.

"Seventeen dollars for a daiquiri!" he says. "You gotta come sometime."

"Are you still in music?" she asks Marty.

"I play around a little," he tells her.

"He still tours," Julius says. "He's got a doo-wop group, they do revival, you gotta hear 'em sometime. And he scores movies. They're filming a big movie over in Brooklyn," Julius says. "Marty's on the set every day."

"That sounds interesting."

Marty shrugs. "I mostly produce for friends, do some mixing." He glances at, then away from her. "Whatever."

They pass one of the decaying old buildings she has wondered about, three stories of smashed windows and graffiti'd brick, a chain-link fence. "What is that, do you know?" she asks. "It's horrible-looking."

"Old age home," says Julius. "Been here forever. They got it shut down, now."

"It's like some Dickensian orphanage."

"Marty, you had someone in there, right? Your uncle?"

"Yeah." He nods. "Old guy. Died in there when I was a kid."

"I'm sorry," Sarah says. "That's so sad." She smiles in sympathy, envisions a lonely old man, abandoned by family and friends, lying on a cot, withering away to the unrelenting sound of seagulls and crashing waves, the smell of aging bodies and industrial disinfectant. Marty doesn't look especially sad, however, or say anything more, and her words sound insipid, hanging there. "So . . . are they going to tear it down?"

"No, they're re-doing it," he says. "It'll be a community center or something. Maybe a new school. There's good stuff coming, here."

"Yeah, he keeps saying." Julius nudges her. "This whole place went to hell a while back. Great when we were kids, but the late sixties, the seventies, you know, economy tanked and people got the hell outta here. I been trying for years to get this guy to move to the city. You gotta move to the city, I keep telling him."

Marty nods good-naturedly.

"He won't budge. Says it's all coming back these days. It's your life, I tell him."

After another hour of walking, Julius says he's hungry. It is now late in the afternoon, the sun has sloped, and it's too late, she thinks regretfully, to paint.

"What's that place you were talking about around here, Marty? The seafood place?" Julius asks.

"Lundy's. But that's in Sheepshead Bay. We go after shooting, sometimes."

"Let's go. You like seafood? I'm starving."

"You know, I've never been to Brooklyn," she says. "I picture it like in movies. *Moonstruck. Goodfellas.* Woody Allen stuff." She glances at Marty, to include him.

"I don't want to eat yet," says Marty.

"You want to come for dinner?" Julius asks her; she hesitates, unsure whether Marty has merely postponed the dinner, or declined his inclusion entirely.

"I don't know . . . I should still get a few hours' work done." There's spinach left, she thinks, and pasta waiting for her. I might open a can of tuna.

"Tell you what, gimme your number, I'll call you in an hour."

"Okay . . . " She scribbles on a page of her sketchpad, rips it off, hands it to him. She wonders if Marty will be hungry in an hour.

"What's this?" Julius asks.

"The phone number."

"This's the house number. My brother, he's married to Rose eighteen years, you think I don't know Pearl's telephone number?" Julius takes the scrap from her and passes it to Marty. "Here. You keep that." Marty shrugs, and puts it in the pocket of his sweatsuit. He nods at her, turns, and strolls away, heading back along the shoreline toward the Rockaway homes. Julius takes out his phone. "Gimme your cell. I'll program it in mine. See? We can do this now. Look how good this works."

Julius doesn't call until seven-thirty, at which point Bernadette and Avery have already taken over the kitchen with some kind of stew, are banging pots, bellowing at and around each other. Julius's first-person pronouns indicate he's coming to pick her up alone. She's hungry, and the yelling in the kitchen is giving her a headache. She decides to go to dinner, but also decides, at least, that she will partly stick to her resolution and not wash her hair. An assertion of indifference.

"Do you know Julius?" she inquires of Avery as he pours out basmati rice from a massive burlap sack he and Bernadette keep in the storeroom off the kitchen.

"Ah, Julius. Yes, he is uncle to Susan, I think. You are going out?" He seems very pleased, relieved almost, that she will not be having her dinner alone.

I have been eating my dinner alone by choice, she wants

to tell him, but says nothing. She just smiles, nods, and exits by the kitchen door to wait outside the house.

"We will be keeping the light on for you, yes?" he booms after her.

⁓

WHEN SHE GETS into Julius's car, a metallic gold Jaguar, she breathes in air freshly sweetened with men's cologne; it troubles her for being as unperfumed as she is, and also for its scent of expectation.

They leave Rockaway, and, as they drive across the Marine Parkway Bridge, he asks her if she's ever been married. She says no, and then decides it's blatantly rude not to return the question.

"Nope. Lived with a lady for twelve years, though. Moira. Irish Catholic girl, there you go. Should find me a nice Jewish girl. Have kids. Not too late for me, huh?"

She smiles, nods, peers out the window. "Hey, Flatbush Avenue," she says. "I guess I am officially in Brooklyn. Looks like a big field."

"Yeah," he says. "We're going through Marine Park now. That's Bennett Field, over there. Lots of famous places around here. I'll drive you by Coney Island, later. Brighton Beach. Better in the day, though."

At Lundy's he propels her to the oyster bar and announces his plan to just begin the evening here, for cocktails and appetizers. A chalkboard listing freshly caught options hangs on fishnet over their heads. Julius orders from the bartender—a guy dressed as a pirate, briskly quartering lemons—vodka martinis and a half dozen each of littleneck and topneck clams, and Wellfleet oysters. She has never heard of Wellfleet and decides to look up their classification in her book when she gets home. Julius cocks back his head and lets an oyster slide from shell to throat; she instead uses her tiny fork to rip free the oyster's last clinging shred and transfer it primly to her mouth.

"They'd make good spoons, wouldn't they?" she says, replacing the empty oyster shell in its berth of crushed ice. "I've been collecting them on the beach. I feel like I'm choosing flatware for my bridal registration."

"What, honey?"

"Oh, nothing." She touches her lips to her martini, and reaches for a littleneck. The oyster pirate brings her another martini at Julius's crooked finger, then, smiling, shucks oyster after oyster. She wonders if he ever cuts himself by accident. She wonders if the lemon juice from all those wedges burns.

He asks if she has any kids, and she tells him No, but she is very close to her parents. They're a very close family. Her parents are just wonderful. They're getting older, though. She tells him her mother is in poor health now, liver problems and maybe a transplant down the road, that her father has just been diagnosed with prostate cancer. But early stage. They are treating it with hormone therapy, she adds, sipping her martini, and are all very hopeful.

"Yeah," he says, nodding enthusiastically. "Hormone therapy. They say that works great, can sometimes do the whole job. Or maybe with the radiation they do. The younger you are, that's when it's bad. But you get hit at sixty-five, seventy, you're okay, you know? Something else's gonna kill you first." He seems contemplative and informed on this subject, and she realizes, after all, that he probably isn't that much younger than her father. "It's nice they got you to depend on now," he adds.

"Yes," she says. "I live, well I *lived*, just down the street. I do their shopping, take them to their appointments, stuff like that. They're fun to cook for. I like to make them special meals, healthy things, you know. Nonfat sour cream. Hide the vegetables."

"See, that's really something, a daughter like you. Really something." He nods approvingly at her, and she smiles, basks a little, then waves away the compliment.

"Oh, they're wonderful. They're doing great. Really strong. They'll both probably live a long, long time, yet." She takes a healthy swallow of martini. "Thank God."

The shrimp cocktail arrives; a rhomboid dish of thick

crimson sauce, the shrimps clinging to its glass rim like drowning people clutching at a lifeboat.

When the check comes she pokes her hand at it, but Julius bemusedly slaps a credit card on top, away from her. The oyster pirate smiles knowingly at her and she understands, with Julius paying for the evening, that she now has a duty to be a charming, attentive companion. She needs to stop discussing stupid and unkind things like prostate cancer and oyster shell bridal spoons. The thought of the rest of the evening still to go like this exhausts her.

"You look a little like Anthony Quinn," she tells him.

"Yeah?" he says, pleased. "Hey, see, then I got time yet. He was still having kids up till the end, right?"

"Right," she assures him. "Never too late for a fresh start."

Before they leave he loudly asks the manager where to go for real Italian food around here; she thinks this is meant to underscore for her that while he once was from here, he is now from Manhattan. The manager snaps up a card from a large clamshell on the counter, scribbles, and hands it to him. "Marino's," he says. "Eighteenth and a hunnert sixty-seven. Ask for Dean. Tell him Larry from Lundy's sent yover."

Julius gets lost. They drive through brightly lit Little Odessa, on a tunnel-like street beneath an elevated train, where they pass pierogi stands selling homemade borscht and Russian nightclubs advertising acts in neon Cyrillic letters. *That* was a great trip, she says, when I was in Russia, and launches into the story of traveling Europe the summer after college, before she was supposed to move to Chicago for grad school, the tour meant to study Balthus's naked little girls at the Pompidou, Goya's witchy women, gouaches in the Prado—she remembers roaming careless and carefree, light-weight everything tossed in a nylon backpack, the gossamer-float sense of skimming trains—and tells him how, the funny thing of the story is, really, that her most vivid memory is standing in line for hours outside the Hermitage to get real Russian vodka, how there turned out to be a glass bottle shortage and so vodka was doled out in condoms, seriously, men rushing home with their drooping latex phalluses of booze, but Julius interrupts to point out Coney Island in an open-ended way, as if expecting her to want to ride the roll-ercoaster. She then tries asking questions about his work in Manhattan, his upcoming trip to Cuba, but finally realizes his constant What, honey?s and What, sweetheart?s in response means he's rather deaf. But he doesn't seem particularly ill at ease with silence, so she stops talking at all.

Marino's is on the other side of Brooklyn, and in the end it takes them fifty silent and cologne'd minutes driving through revolving strips of Ethiopian, Russian, Italian, Has-sidic, and Puerto Rican neighborhoods to get there. To her dismay, they are told there will be a forty-five minute wait, but Julius hands Larry-from-Lundy's card to the maître d' to give to Dean, and they are immediately seated in the prime booth of a black and pink Art Deco room with vertical strips of mirror on the walls. Julius pre-orders the chocolate soufflé, requests another round of martinis, which, when they arrive, he announces inferior to martinis in the city. It's the vodka, he tells her, they try to pass off the cheap stuff. He lists better restaurants in Manhattan he will take her to. Over the penne arrabiata he inquires with circuitous and excessive delicacy how old she is and then seems both surprised and disappointed at almost-thirty-five; she feels briefly guilty, as though she'd deliberately sought to tantalize with the false impression of fertility and youth. She re-assures him of her ability to impersonate twenty-something with the story of how she still gets carded in supermarkets when she buys wine. He seems cheered and charmed, too, by the fact that she purchases her wine in supermarkets, and promptly orders three glasses of the restaurant's finest cabernets, in order to cultivate her palate. She pretends to be able to discern a difference and insists on drinking down the three glasses by herself, to avoid his getting drunk and aggressive or getting them killed on the drive home. When she asks how old he is, he coyly tells her the year of his birth and makes her do the math.

Fifty-seven, she figures. No, fifty-eight.

"Most shells have a life span of about two to fifteen years," she says. "The larger ones live longer, they can make it up to seventy-five." My father is only sixty-six, she thinks.

"What, sweetheart?"

"Thank you very much for dinner," she says loudly.

"Yeah, pretty lucky I found you out there today, on the beach," he says, looking happy. "Thought that was probably you, sitting there. I knocked at the door, but no one was home. Pretty lucky." She doesn't point out the lack of luck involved—that if she hadn't been sitting on the beach, she likely would've been in the house. She decides to let him think he has found something.

When he offers her a sip of his after-dinner Frangelico she gulps three times.

Her seatbelt is unbuckled five houses down from Nana's, and when he slows then stops the car she leans in quickly to peck him on the cheek; he clasps the back of her head with his abalone-thick hand, holding her face against his for an extra moment.

"You want to maybe have dinner Friday? I'll know to-morrow if Cuba's happening this week or not, I'll call you."

She hurries into bed without toothbrushing or face-washing; his cologne, cloying and stale, she finds when she awakens in the morning, has transferred from his face to her cheek, to her pillow, to her sweater, and drifts through the rest of the house, mingling with the curry for days.

SHE LOOKS FOR mussel shells. Most are broken; all have been snapped into halves. After two hours' search she comes upon a perfect, intact bivalve; its sides are still held together by a fragile, drying ligament, but strained apart, gapped like castanets or a Munchean scream. She peers inside, but any trace of meat is long gone. There is something mythological here, something insightful and interesting; she remembers what she thinks is a Greek philosopher's theory of male and female halves, once joined together in human form, now split apart in two drifting, searching sexes. She examines the empty and strained shell, noting its creamy nacre is worn from exposure, its hard beryline surface starting to fade, its chipped edges, its halves shaped like swollen, elongated tears. She hurries the mussel home. By the time she's rinsing sand from her feet on the front porch she can't conjure up what beauty or resonance she saw in the shell, only that it's lusterless, and tacky with dry salt, and so decides instead to first make herself some scrambled eggs for lunch. Also, her head is pounding, from sparing Julius all that alcohol the night before, and so she opens a bottle of beer.

She passes through the cool dark hallways of the house, climbs the creaking stairs—Why does Nana need all these family photos everywhere? she thinks—to her corner bedroom, winces at the sudden glare of sun through all those windows. She has already made the bed, as she has conscientiously done every morning, stretching the chenille coverlet smooth. She has already put yesterday's clothes in the hamper, already tidied the bathroom and aligned her toiletries and hung her towels, and neatly laid out her brushes on the nightstand. She has already swept up the traces of sand that always seem to creep into her room, despite the careful rinsing of her feet when she enters the house from the beach.

All right, she thinks. You're all ready to begin. She selects a canvas, positions it perfectly on her easel. *Mytilus edulis*, she thinks, looking at her gaping shell. The common blue mussel. She seizes a tube of pthalo blue, punctures it open.

There. You have begun.

Then dioxazine purple. Aureolin yellow, viridian, ivory, iron oxide black. She studies the moist little squeezings of color on her palette. Even with the employee discount she'd spent a fortune on these studio-sized tubes in her wooden case: Old Holland, the best. Excellent strength of color and lightfastness, no cheap fillers, their pigments still fine-ground by old-fashioned stone rollers and mixed with cold-pressed, sun-bleached virgin linseed oil, each tube packed by hand. She has recited that to customers for over ten years, using her old college canvases as example and display, and, before quitting, purchased herself this grand spectrum. She must be careful not to waste them, all these rich colors.

The sun through a picture window reflects off the virgin canvas in a harsh, hurtful way. A blank canvas is awful, an insult, she thinks. A sin. You must overcome the sin of the blank canvas.

She seizes a brush. It is a ragged, windy day; sand flecks the window glass and the wooden frames are rattling in their sockets. She sets the brush down, contemplates the mussel, its faint pearlescence, then, determined, punctures one more tube and squeezes out a healthy dollop of rose dore madder. She picks up a palette knife, dips its edge, taps, makes pretty red dots on the palette. Like smallpox, she thinks. Measles. A coughed spray of consumptive blood. Focus, Sarah, she tells herself. Stop playing around. Carpe diem yourself. Seize this opportunity to express and define who you are, now. Fresh start.

She puts the palette knife down, swigs beer, and looks out toward the ocean. A seagull hangs, floats in reverse for a moment, fighting the wind, then flies away beyond her view. At the seam of horizon and sea is a large ship, a tanker, she decides, or some kind of freighter. A liner, maybe a cruise vessel. She thinks of buying an illustrated book about ships, all the different kinds. The ship slowly crosses the three picture windows, absorbing the afternoon. When her cell phone rings, once, then twice, she doesn't answer it. You should have at least sketched the ship, she thinks, too late, as it passes from her last framed view. She gets up, rinses her unused brushes in naphtha in her bathroom sink, props them head-up in jars to dry. She scrapes the red from her knife, wipes it, sets her palette aside. The image of a ship, perfect in its wandering free, floating ship-ness. A floating seagull. Or the ocean itself, the view from your window, the waves and all that beautiful sky. A simple seascape. You should just paint whatever you see, at the moment, in the moment, to get you started. Set you on the path. Why don't you just do that? Like a prompt. Yes, that's what you'll do. She rips from *A Collector's Guide to Seashells of the World* several color plates of the more florid, exotic shells and scotch-tapes them, careful not to give herself paper cuts, over the framed photos of Nana Pearl's family hung in groupings on the walls of her room.

The humming, relentless sound of breaking waves is beginning to get on her nerves. It is starting to feel as if two conch shells are clamped on her head, trapping the sea's whispery rise and falls against her ears.

⁓

"IT IS ENJOYABLE for me to watch you cook," says Ber-nadette with pleasure. "It is so different from Sri Lankan cooking."

"Yeah, that's true," replies Sarah, unsure of what else to say. As she continues ribboning a roasted red pepper, Ber-nadette conscientiously snaps off the kitchen light.

"Could you leave that on?" Sarah asks politely. "I mean, I know it's still pretty light out, but this is sort of a sharp knife."

"Oh, yes, I am sorry." Bernadette, lugging in the burlap bag of basmati rice, snaps the light back on. "You are having trouble with your eyes?"

"No, no, they're fine. I'd just hate to cut myself, you know."

"I have cataracts," Bernadette informs her loudly. "Next month I am going home to Sri Lanka for the surgery."

"Really?" I'll have the house to myself, Sarah thinks. Good, easier to focus that way.

"And for my teeth, too." Bernadette taps her upper lip with a finger. "I am losing so many teeth, here."

"I'm sorry. Do you really have to fly back to do all of that?"

"It is less money for me at home."

"Ah." Sarah nods sympathetically. She feels reproachable for her sound teeth, her waste of light.

"But it will be good for visiting my family," Bernadette says, measuring rice into a saucepan. "My daughter Nissa is graduating from school as a doctor."

"That's great. Congratulations. You must be really proud."

"And my daughter Celeste has the new little boy I have not seen yet. It makes me lonely for him."

"You must miss them," Sarah says. How can someone be lonely for someone they've never met? she thinks.

"Yes," Bernadette says cheerfully. "Very much. I will show you photographs?"

"Sure, yeah."

"It is hard for a mother, when she is not with her children. Even when they are grown, and off living their own lives. But, perhaps it not as hard for the child?" She looks at Sarah, a small, closed-lipped, questioning smile that makes her nervous.

"Oh, I don't know about that," she says. "I miss my parents. I mean, of course I miss them. That's totally normal, right?"

Bernadette adds a stream of cloudy water to her rice, sets the pan on the stove. "And how is your painting coming? It is happy for you, being here?"

"It's great. I'm getting so much done. The open air, all the light. The quiet . . . "

"Avery and I were discussing this. We would love to see your work."

"Well, that's really nice of you guys, thank you, but—"

"But an artist must be ready to do this. It must be the right time, for showing the work to others. We understand."

"Yeah. Exactly. But sometime, sure. Thanks." She puts her knife down in the sink, scoops her red pepper on top of her pasta.

"Ah, you are having that on your noodles? I see."

"Oh, let me get out of your way, now," Sarah says quickly, taking her plate upstairs to her room.

THE HOUSE PHONE rings the next day as she's slicing strawberries for her afternoon snack. After this, she thinks, you will take a good, vigorous walk on the beach, before that fog comes in. Get your blood moving. And then you will get to work. Get productive, take full advantage of this important—

"Hello?"

"Is this Sarah?"

"Yes?"

"It's Marty. You know, Julius's friend."

"Oh. Hi."

"I'm having shabbes dinner with friends tonight, they live down the street from you."

"Uh huh."

"It's the last night of Passover, too."

"Oh, yeah, that's right. Damn, I forgot." She suddenly pictures her parents, going through the motions of a seder without her, alone. A lonely lamb shank, two hard-boiled eggs. Store-bought gefilte fish, a sad, sodium-filled can of chicken soup. Waiting for her to call and check in, *Happy Pesach, Mom and Dad!* Or maybe they didn't even bother having a seder this year, with her gone. She sees them sitting alone at the kitchen table, eating one of the low-fat casseroles she'd prepared, labeled, stocked their freezer with. She feels sad, guilty, the dull start of a headache, doesn't hear the silence on the line, and then:

"Well, you want to come or what?" His voice is softer, freer of Brooklyn than Julius's.

"Um . . . I'm just putting my dinner in the oven."

"Take it out."

She thinks of her greasy hair, her still-unwashed body. "What time?"

"Not till seven-thirty or eight. We're still shooting. I'll pick you up."

"Okay. Not before seven-thirty," she says, calculating.

"It's shabbes, Sarah. We can't eat before eight, anyway."

He hangs up, and she figures if she cuts short her walk she'll have plenty of time to shower and dress for dinner, to do her hair. She'll come up with a new ritual to inspire the perfect painting. No more chocolate, maybe. Or no more wine, that's good, be disciplined, keep your head clear, yes.

<hr />

HE IS DRESSED nicely in black jeans and a linen shirt, his jaw shaved free of bristle, but still wears the black knit cap.

"We're walking?" she asks, following him down the sidewalk.

"They only live a few blocks over. I walked here."

They cross the main boulevard, away from the fancier oceanfront properties and the darkening eastern sky, wind through the neighborhood of modest homes pressing close to the street, children's toys and aluminum lawn chairs left out on porches, bathing suits hung out to dry. They pass families walking along, on their way to synagogue, she assumes, from their yarmulkes and dark suits, the women dressed in long sleeves, long skirts, hats or fancy scarves covering their heads. Even the children, solemn and formally dressed, walking beside their parents like tiny sedate adults.

"So, who are these people? Where we're going?"

"Itzak and Darlene, their kids. Itzak and I grew up together."

"Like you and Julius?"

"No, I knew Julius later. Itzak and me, we used to steal Abba Zabbas from the dime store, you know? Cut school and go smoke grass. Sneak out to the city, go to the clubs. That was music. You ever hear of the Cedar Bar? The Village Vanguard?"

"No."

"No? Wow. Early, mid-sixties, Itzak and me, we're just kids, right? We're maybe fifteen, sixteen, we're sneaking into these basement clubs, we're hearing Al Cohn, Howard Hart. Miles Davis. Wild."

"I've heard of Miles Davis," she says.

"Itzak's Hasidic now. Really beautiful."

"Oh?" Who is this person? she thinks. What am I doing here? "I feel funny, not bringing anything. I'm a bad guest."

"You could've brought the wrong thing, though. Even the wine, it has to be kosher."

"I thought of that. I would've brought a bag of oranges, or something."

He shrugs. "Hey, whatever."

She feels dismissed, somehow. Irrelevant. "So . . . when did you start keeping kosher? Julius said it was a new thing for you?"

"Couple of years ago."

"Sort of a . . . " she is about to say *midlife crisis*, but stops herself, " . . . spiritual awakening?"

"I had stuff to figure out. Think about."

"Looking for answers?"

"Looking for questions." He smiles, nods at a young couple pushing a stroller. "*Shabbat Shalom*," he tells them, and they smile, murmur back: "*Chag Sameach*."

"See, that's nice," he says quietly to Sarah. "All the young people living here now. They're moving back and settling down, starting their own families. We got all these kids growing up here together, the Jewish kids, the Irish and the Hispanic and black kids, they're all out on the playground. The old people, they sit and watch. Everyone going to shul or church on Sunday morning. A real community. It's beautiful. It's got this energy, you know? When people come together like that."

"It's so different from where I grew up. Nobody talked to anybody. Everybody just drives around in their car."

"So, this is good for you, yeah?"

"Oh sure," she says. "You can really feel the energy here. Like you said.

He nods. She doesn't know what else to say. They walk in silence, as she feels the fog limpen her hair.

———

ITZAK LOOKS LIKE an Old World photograph of someone's dead great-grandfather, in blacks and beiges, elaborately yarmulke'd, with sepia-tinted teeth and long gray beard wispy as a cirrus cloud. The house is decorated with Judaica. Sarah expects his wife to be shrouded and bewigged and haggard from childbearing, but Darlene is trimly dressed in a sleeveless blouse and slacks, with her own curly bobbed hair. Their teenage son Jonah is wearing a Nine Inch Nails T-shirt, and joke-pleads with his father about the promise of a new videogame; their daughter Gwen, skinny and miniskirted, her right ear triple-pierced, is a freshman at NYU, studying psychology. They invite Sarah to sit in the place of honor and she readies herself, steels herself for the endless and obligatory ritual—*Why matzoh? Why bitter herbs? Why do we recline?*—but there is no wine-stained Haggadah in sight, no painstaking array of bitter herbs and chopped apple-and-nuts; the family simply sings in Hebrew one quick and ebullient prayer she doesn't know, and Itzak announces That's it, everybody, let's eat!

Everyone troops happily to the kitchen sink to wash their hands. Back at the table Itzak passes her a plate of matzoh and she readies herself again, for the hurrying-from-bondage-and-Pharaoh's-troops lecture (lamb's blood smeared on doors, gross), the ten plagues that always creeped her out as a child (pestilence, boils, locusts, darkness and tragedy and despair to be visited upon their house at any moment), but Itzak's discussion of matzoh is Freudian: The unleavened bread, he says, symbolizes the suppression of human ego. Risen bread, puffed up with yeast and air, shows the swelling of ego, the human soul presumptuous before God. Gwen proclaims all religious ecstasy—any type of religious faith, she argues, actually—to be merely a form of psychological repression if not outright delusion, which Jonah—apparently planning on rabbinical school—takes good-natured issue with, and as the debate continues and floats over her head and beyond her, Sarah quickly drinks down the glass of kosher wine Itzak has poured for her—an exception to the rule, but she's never tasted kosher wine, is curious, although there is no discernible difference in taste from regular wine, she thinks—then is too embarrassed to ask for more. Always plenty of wine, at home, at least. The Kiddush, the blessing of the wine, fill that cup again, by all means.

Marty ignores her during dinner, listens nodding to the family's textbook-and-Torah-peppered deliberations, and cracks the matzoh in his teeth. Darlene finally brings out a macaroon-ringed platter of fruit for dessert but before the last of the pineapple is tugged from its husk, Marty wanders from the table. Sarah feels confused, then resentful, unsure whether she should remain with her hosts, or follow. She excuses herself to go to the bathroom.

She finds him on the living room couch, reading in *Newsday* about a Texas couple on death row, both about to be executed for killing their two children.

"Ah, family life," she says brightly. He frowns a little at her and she realizes he thinks she's being snide about his friends. "No, *that* family," she adds, tapping the headline.

"Yeah, look at that. Terrible. What about you?" He puts the paper aside.

"My family? No, we haven't killed each other yet," she says.

He looks at her, not seeming to get the joke. "Yeah? That's it?"

"Well, it's just my parents. My family. They're in San Diego."

He nods.

"Actually," she says, "well, I had a younger brother. But he died."

He blinks at her. "Wow."

"Yeah. When he was really little."

"What happened?"

"Meningitis. He was almost four."

"Oh, man. I'm sorry."

"Thanks. His name was Aaron. But it was a long time ago, so . . . " Butter blond hair, toddler diapers, sticky hands. Smiling parents. She clears her throat. "I hardly even remember him." Baby clothes in blues: robin's egg, turquoise, cerulean sky.

"That's terrible. A terrible thing for parents."

"I know." She nods.

"'Cause that's really just, *it*, you know? Family, kids. Why we do any of it. That's what keeps us going." He tilts his head toward the dining room. "Like in there. Beautiful."

"Yeah." I could go back and eat pineapple, she thinks. I could just go home. Her eye catches Itzak, in the dining room, setting out a bottle of brandy and several tiny glasses. It will look bad if she suddenly rushes back in there, now. "So, for something like that," she asks, tapping the newspaper again, "where do you stand?" She sits deliberately at the other end of the sofa.

"Stand on what?"

"The death penalty. Eye for an eye? Blood atonement?"

He ponders for her, scratching at his black knit cap. "I guess you could argue either side, you know?"

"Just keep questioning, right?"

"Yeah. That's the thing."

"I thought you'd have a strong opinion about it. Either way. You know, vengeful God, benevolent God . . . "

He shrugs. "Whatever."

"You say that a lot. 'Whatever.'"

"I do?"

"It's so dismissive."

"What do you mean?"

"It's like you're not only wiping out what you've just said, you're erasing anything the other person said, too. You're dismissing any connection. Like, 'why bother?'" She demonstrates, contemptuously, dismissively waving a hand. "Whatever."

"Huh. You're right."

"Not that I took it personally," she says, realizing how in saying that she is exhibiting exactly the opposite.

"No, thank you. This is good you're telling me this. You're very insightful."

She suddenly feels ridiculous. She looks away from him and picks up a book tucked in the cushion gap of the sofa: *The Torah Anthology*. She opens it to the middle and focuses on rituals for purifying the leprosy of the soul, trying to convey that he should return to his newspaper and do the same. He continues to study her. She wonders what his head is like under the knit cap—thready hair, bald scalp, scars, freckles? She wonders how old he is. He must be around

Julius's age, she figures, if they were teenage buddies. She has a sudden, mean urge to discuss prostate cancer.

"What's that?" he asks.

"What?"

"That." He points to her right hand turning a page. "That."

"Oh," she says. "That. It's nothing." She sets the paper down, covers with her left hand the crescent ridge of scar embracing her right thumb joint. "Nothing. Old kitchen accident. I was cutting a bagel." She thinks this is funny, but again he doesn't seem to get the joke. "People don't usually notice it," she tells him. "It isn't very noticeable." She smoothes down the long sleeves of her blouse, crosses her arms.

"How did your painting go today?" he asks.

She shrugs. "Bad day."

"What's a bad day?"

"Not getting any work done. I just wandered around. Ate some strawberries. Wasted time."

"Why is that a waste?"

"Well, this is such a big opportunity. Being here. Having all this time to myself, this whole summer to focus on my work, no job or anything. And, you know, tick tick tick. I shouldn't just be . . . strolling around. I mean, my parents rely on me a lot, and I'm not there. I'm here, just doing the melancholy-artist-on-the-beach thing. I am a strolling, wandering cliché." He nods at her, but it is thoughtful nodding, not affirming. "I might as well be at home," she adds. "If I'm not going to be more . . . oh, I don't know."

"You worry about them. You take care of them. That's nice."

"I try. I do what I can. It's not like they need nursing care, anything like that. Although my dad doesn't like my mom driving anymore, so I'm sort of on call when she has errands or something. And he doesn't eat like he's supposed to, with his heart, we're always arguing about his food. I do their bills and stuff. But they're pretty self-sufficient. They're doing fine. I would never have left them alone to come here, otherwise."

"Yeah, sure." His face is thoughtful, and she feels a rush of guilt. He must think she's terrible, abandoning her parents this way.

"And I made sure they had phone numbers to call if they need any help. I'm sure they'll be fine. There's a Jewish Family Services they can call. And they have neighbors. But they won't. I mean, they like it when I'm there to do stuff. They're used to how I do stuff for them. As opposed to some stranger coming in to help."

"That's beautiful."

"Well, I do my best. They're my parents." She shrugs again. "What're you going to do, right?"

"But there's stuff you need to do for you now."

"I guess."

"Your stuff's important. You got this big exhibit happening, you're going out in the world with all that."

She nods, surprised he remembered.

"The problem," he says, "is that you are way too hard on yourself."

"No," she says. "The problem is I am not nearly hard *enough* on myself." She has said this before, to many people, and it is meant to be charmingly self-abnegating, said with a meek smile. But the fresh-cut truth of it stings unexpectedly. Her jaw suddenly feels unhinged in its joints; she realizes, mortified, that she is about to cry. She clenches her teeth.

"Why did that upset you?" he asks gently.

"I'm not upset," she says. Itzak should call us back into the dining room, she thinks. He should be offering brandy to his guests.

"Give yourself time. Okay, yeah, so it's cliché, I know, but it's like an oyster." He holds up his hands to form an oyster. "It has to start with that tiny speck of sand inside, right? It starts with practically nothing. Then layers and layers, growing a pearl. It takes time. You have to allow yourself that."

"Did you know that oysters are hermaphroditic?" she asks.

"Huh. No, I didn't know that." He seems amused, at last. "I don't eat oysters. You ever do acid?" he asks.

"I don't like hallucinogenics."

"Why not?"

"I don't want my brain getting away from me like that. Running loose in the store."

"We're more than our rational mind. That's not all we are."

"Ah. The 'soul,' right? The divine spark? Breath of God."

"Yeah, that's what's great about tripping. You get there. That pure place. You strip away that layer of intellect, that conscious wall you build around yourself. It's like peeling the scum off pudding, you get at the good stuff, where it's all messy and warm. Where it's real."

"I bet you've done a *lot* of acid," she says, smiling.

"Why do you think that?"

"You're a musician."

"Maybe. Acid, hash, mushrooms. I like mushrooms. Hey," he says, waving a hand—he is about to end with *whatever*, but he sees her smiling, and stops. "Sure," he says instead. "I've done my share."

"Is it hard to find kosher acid?" she asks, and he finally smiles back.

"There's lots of kinds of Jews," he says. "Like this, here. I didn't want you to miss Pesach."

"Thanks," she says. "This one was definitely different." She glances at the crescent scar on her hand, folds her hands away in her lap. *Why is this night different from any other?* she thinks.

"You do the whole thing, at home? With your family?"

"Oh, sure. Well, when I was little. It'd be crazy for weeks. I mean, happy-crazy, you know. We aren't very religious, but still. It was a big production. Everyone had their own job to do, all of us . . . " Her mother, chopping the apples. Boiling a chicken. The smell of silver polish, a hot iron steaming the afikomen cloth. Her mother promising a spoonful of honey if Sarah will try, just *try*, the homemade chopped liver, *Show your brother what a big girl his sister is*, then she is chuckling, laughing, as Sarah pretends to choke, to gag, to writhe dyingly on the floor. *All right, here's your honey, honey! Now you go set the table, Sarah Bernhardt!* Her father is presiding at dinner, slicing the brisket, he is joke-threatening they'll do the whole service *Word for Hebrew word if everyone doesn't stop laughing!* while joke-sneaking bits of meat from the platter, stuffing his mouth with big gobbling noises to make everyone laugh even more. This year is special, this year she is prompting her little brother on the Four Questions, *Why is this night different from any other?*, it's his turn now, he is just old enough, Aaron, the youngest child, and he is giggling, delighted with the new role, all the big responsibility. Everyone is so proud of him, clapping. She hides the afikomen matzoh for him, under the stuffed panda pillow on his bed to make it easy, there it is, *He found it, give Aaron the prize, Daddy!* All of them applauding, celebrating, together.

"We all did it together," she says. "The big whole family thing, yeah."

"That's nice. Tradition."

"Not really. I mean, it didn't have *time* to be tradition. To become that. Because then Aaron died. You know, my little brother?" He nods solemnly. "And afterward, that first year, my parents weren't doing very well. My dad was working a lot, all the time. Or playing golf. And my mom slept half the day, then she'd get up and have these terrible headaches and go right back to bed. And the TV was always on, like this white humming noise always in the background, they'd just sit there facing it every night for hours. I don't think they were even watching, or listening. Just zoned out. Not talking. I'm sure it was a coping thing, you know?"

"Yeah, sure."

"I mean, *now* I can look back and understand. They were depressed. They were devastated. That kind of grief. It broke them. But when you're a little kid, and your parents just go zombie, right? What do you do? So that first Passover after Aaron died, I realized it wasn't going to happen, you know, because *why bother*? That's what my dad kept saying, about everything. 'Why even bother?' So I got the idea I'd do it. I'd do the whole thing, surprise them, you know? Make them feel better."

"That was sweet of you."

"Right, like a seder's going to make up for everything." She laughs. "So I made the soup, which means I 'doctored up' some broth from a can. And I got that gefilte fish in the jar with the jelly and that bright pink horseradish and I bought one of those ready-roasted chickens in the bag and got out the silver and set the table, the whole thing. I wanted it to be perfect. My friend Emily's mom Leah, you know, one of Nana Pearl's daughters?"

"Yeah."

"She took me to the store for all the stuff. And she even bought the wine for me, and I did the whole service, with all the prayers and courses. And I drew a special Passover picture of us. 'Our Family Seder.' To go on the fridge. I had this huge megabox of crayons, you know, a dozen shades of every color?" Burgundy, scarlet, crimson, cerise. "I really went to town on that drawing. Jewish iconography and everything." Waxy lamb's blood scribbled on the door. Fool the Angel of Death that way, or was that Pharaoh's troops? Pass over this house, spare the first-born son.

"They must've loved all that."

"It was pretty awful, actually." She sees her mother, numbly drinking the wine, her father's eyes on some muted game on the television over her head. She hears herself reading from the Haggadah, the sound of her own thin little voice in the quiet, quiet room.

Why is this night different from any other night?

Back to being her turn again, her job. The youngest child, only child.

"It was so awful. I oversalted the soup, I even burned the chicken trying to heat it up. The kitchen was full of smoke, that dark gray burn smoke, you could smell it all through dinner. You could smell it for days."

Locusts, pestilence. Darkness visited upon the house.

"I bet they didn't care about that," he says, gently.

"And my mom, when she saw the drawing, she just started to cry. And then my dad's face . . . I'd drawn the three of us. The Mommy, the Daddy, and me"—*Mommy, Daddy, come see, come look*—"all holding hands. Just us three. Big mistake. In hindsight."

She remembers clearing the dishes, leaving her mother and father in their weeping and silence at the dining room table, throwing the half-eaten food in the kitchen trash. She remembers throwing her drawing in after, dumping the garish, uneaten horseradish on top of all the crayoned shine. She remembers cleaning everything up, standing at the sink and washing dishes, rinsing out the soup can, everything soapy, slippery, gripping the can hard, remembers the jagged lip of the metal lid making its quick crescent slice, the well of blood into the gray dishwater, a sudden rich cloud of red brightening it all up.

Lamb's blood, the small sacrifice. She stands, watching, opens her mouth to cry, to call her mother or father to help, *Mommy, Daddy, come see, come look, I need you*, but then doesn't. *Mommy, Daddy, help me, it hurts*. She just stands there, quiet, still, watches the pretty red blossom and float until her mother comes in to pour herself the last of the wine and sees, says *What did you do to yourself, Sarah? Go, go get yourself a Band-Aid, go on.* A ridge of scar tissue, now, crudely healed. They should have taken me for stitches, she thinks. Why didn't they take me for stitches?

"But I was just a kid, you know . . . " she finishes.

"How old were you?"

"Hmm?" She looks up at him.

"When you did that? The seder?"

"Oh . . . nine, I guess? Maybe ten?"

"Wow." He looks surprised.

"So, now I've done it every year since. The whole routine. I even do the Four Questions. And I wrap up a piece of matzoh and hide it for myself. Then I make my dad give me a dollar."

"You're kidding." He shakes his head. "Wow," he says again.

"Hey, I'm still the youngest child! That dollar is mine!" She laughs. "I know. It's twisted. But that's the tradition now. And once that kind of thing takes, it's too late, right? You're trapped. You're stuck."

"No, see, that's not true. Traditions can change. They're supposed to. They're living things. Always evolving."

"Oh, things've evolved," she says, mock-assuring. "I'm a much better cook now. Chicken soup from scratch."

"No, look, this year, you're here. Right?"

"Right."

"So Pesach is all new again for you, this way. You can appreciate it all over again, like it's the first time. You gotta do that with everything. You can't just move through life, we gotta *recreate* life at the same time. Be conscious of doing that, every single moment."

"Oh my God, that is *so* exhausting." She smiles at him, to soften the comment, then: "I'm kidding. I get it. You're exactly right, this year was definitely different." She waves vaguely at the house, at the family in the dining room.

"And it's good, right?"

"Sure. It's been a blast."

"No, I mean how's it *feel*? How's it different on the *inside*?" He touches his chest. "Like deeper, how?"

She feels impatient. Exhausted, yes, ready for this whole evening to be over with and done. No more questions, please. "Like you said, change is good. This has been a good, conscious, evolving evening. Really. Thank you." She picks up *The Torah Anthology* again. "It's like you're always lifting up rocks to see what's crawling around," she can't resist adding.

He looks at her, bewildered. "We're just talking, here."

She flips pages of purification rituals. "You're like those people on the beach that're always prying open oysters because maybe maybe there's that pearl inside."

"I am?"

"Or a clam or mussel, like there's going to be some little animal alive in there, but there never is. It's just a shell."

"Is that what you're scared of?"

"I'm not scared. Where do you get that?" She feels fully exasperated now. What's with him, all this interrogation? No, she realizes, she's not exasperated. She feels embarrassed. Too seen-into, too revealed. Your own fault, Sarah, offering up so much personal stuff. No reason to tell him all of that, you don't even know this guy. "You know, I'm just tired. Really. What time is it, anyway?" she asks, standing. Marty doesn't answer, just nods, chewing his lip, and she heads back toward the dining room.

"Sarah," says Itzak. "Come, join us. Have some of this." He smiles at her, carding smooth the fibers of his beard with one hand and offering her a breast-shaped snifter of brandy with the other. "And come every Friday for shabbes. You're always welcome."

Walking the seven blocks by five blocks back to the house in the nighttime dark, passing again all those families heading home now from synagogue, the sleepy children carried in their parents' arms, Sarah and Marty talk politely about movies and fog. She murmurs enthusiastic thanks fifteen feet from the front door, and darts into the house without kissing him on the cheek.

THE NEXT MORNING while munching toast and browsing through *A Collector's Guide to Seashells of the World*, Sarah doodles an idea of a shell on the sports section of *Newsday*, which she is using as a placemat, just below her coffee mug's damp brown ring. It is not a very identifiable shell, nothing pictured in the book, perhaps some kind of generic gastropod. She looks at it a moment, then sketches in the gastropod's little foot, peering out. She is using the black ballpoint pen Bernadette keeps for phone messages, and it blobs a bit, messing things up. She dumps her crumbs on top of the shell and sports section and scoops it all into the box Avery uses for recyclable paper.

She is low on food. Last night's fog is gone, and the sun is a white blister; she puts on her sunglasses, pedals into town on the little-girl bike, and buys: milk, broccoli, tuna, pasta. Olive oil. A bag of oranges, and, why not, a box of unpresumptuous and probably stale matzoh. She has the casual thought of purchasing kosher wine or brandy, maybe for a future shabbes gift, but there is none in the grocery store. She buys a regular kind of table wine, a half-gallon of red, tucks it in her backpack.

On her way home, produce and matzoh shaking in her basket, the heavy bottle between her shoulder blades throwing her slightly off-balance, the bicycle turns off the boulevard and down a street that leads to the beach, several blocks from Nana's. Why not? she thinks again. There's no hurry to get home. It's a pretty day to pedal around. Check out the neighborhood a little more. Be conscious of this beautiful day, appreciate it, fine. The weather is warming; down beyond the end of the street, out on the beach she sees what looks like a bathing-suited family spreading out towels near the still-empty lifeguard chair, or maybe it's a couple of sibling teenagers babysitting a toddler. Maybe I'll go swimming later, she thinks, maybe it'll be warm enough to be okay. Should've bought some ginger ale. In the gaps between houses she spots a few back porch decks, a barbecue, an inflated plastic wading pool, laundry flapping on lines. She rides up and down the length of the street, the bicycle jolting over cracks, looking for a hanging black sweatsuit or jeans. She starts to feel slightly ridiculous, like an ice cream truck circling in desperate search of customers.

Behind a small brick and clapboard house facing the beach she spots a clothesline with dark, drooping squares and rectangles, and the smaller smudge of a hat-sized black dot. She fumbles to take off her sunglasses and the bicycle wobbles; she overcompensates by overjerking the handles, and the front tire flips sideways as if kicked. She falls, skidding, to the asphalt, landing first on one knee, then on her back, the bicycle collapsed and *plinging* on top of her. Oranges roll across the street.

When she can gasp out a breath again, it comes as crying. Her pants are torn; her ripped knee stings and bleeds grit, her shoulder feels shoved through her chest, and she hears the thick clink of broken glass in her backpack. A garnet trickle slowly pools beneath her. She cries in pain and humiliation and hatred. No one comes rushing from the house with the black knit cap hanging on the line. She stills her crying, swallows it down. She slowly gets up on her feet, righting the bicycle. Her sunglasses are tangled in the rear tire's spokes and she has to free them before she limps away, pushing the warped bike before her with raw-scraped hands.

———

AVERY HAS VISED to the kitchen counter an odd propeller-type device and is gripping a coconut in one hand as Sarah enters the kitchen. At the stove, Bernadette is cooking what looks like pita bread on a spatula-style pan. They look at her, puzzled.

"You are all right? What has happened?"

"I wiped out a little on the bike. It's fine, I'm okay."

"You are bleeding that much?" He raises his eyebrows at the ruby splotches on her T-shirt, her pants.

"No, I'm fine. I just spilled something. A juice bottle broke. Really, don't worry, I'm fine."

He seems satisfied, unconcerned. Bernadette looks at Sarah's knee and shakes her head, smiling, then returns to her cooking. Sarah opens her backpack and carefully places the broken wine bottle, piece by piece, into the recycling bin for glass. She hopes they don't smell the alcohol. But they're busy cooking, Bernadette cupping white flour from a canister into a mound of shredded coconut, stirring.

"What are you making?" Sarah asks.

"Bread," Bernadette says happily. She flips a flat disc of it in the pan to its other side. Avery squats on the floor, taps at the equator of his coconut with a hammer and screw-driver-as-chisel, then gives it one hard *thwack*; the coconut cracks perfectly in half, split to symmetrical and concave whiteness. He presses a coconut cup against the propeller blades and cranks a handle; shreds of coconut drift down to the counter like snow, like a pile of pure, dry sand.

"I love coconut," Sarah says.

"You would like to taste?" Bernadette offers her a piece fresh from the stove; it is warm, it smells toasted and rich.

"Sure. Thank you." Sarah chews on the bread; it is delicious. She rinses her torn palms at the sink and pours herself a glass of milky tap water, while Avery shreds out the second coconut shell and Bernadette pats flat another disc of bread. She drinks her water, waiting and hoping for Bernadette to offer her another piece of the bread, but she does not.

Halfway up the stairs to her room Sarah stops and returns to the kitchen. Avery and Bernadette glance silently at her like all the other family eyes in the house, as she digs through the trash bag of recyclable paper and fishes out her little sketch of an insignificant inky shell on the crumbed and coffee-ringed newspaper. She takes the drawing up to her room with her and sits, tracing it with a finger, studying the blank canvas on her easel, while her knee dulls to healing and outside the picture window the glassy acid-green waves break with their rushing, hushing sound and stretch to foam on the sand.

PLAYLAND

"I TALKED TO Julius this morning," says Marty.

"Oh? Is he coming today?"

"No, he had to work."

"On Saturday?" Sarah asks.

"Yeah, I know. It's terrible. You shouldn't work on Saturday." He puts on a pair of dark glasses and glances at himself in the car's rearview mirror. He settles his fedora to a tilt. It is lintless, and spanking black, a new variation on the black knit caps, the baseball caps, the embroidered, Rasta-looking yarmulkes she has seen him wear.

They are driving to Brooklyn, to pick up his musician buddies, then heading to some family park upstate, in Rye, a few hours' drive from Rockaway. Come, he'd said to her on the phone. He and the guys had a gig. An Oldies celebration, WCBS 101.1 FM, New York's Oldies station, live broadcast, she'd get a kick out of it. Marty Zale & the Satellites, he and the guys, going back a long time, twenty years they've been doing this, just for the fun. You oughtta come, you'll have fun, come.

She'd professed great reluctance—I'm really on track with my new painting now, I don't want to break the momentum, she told him—but finally gave in, pleased by his insistence. Her little sketch of a shell has made it onto a canvas in her room; it is now a few charcoal strokes, some vague, preliminary daubs of ivory and iron oxide black. She likes its clumsy little shell foot, just peeking out. It is a slow but good beginning, she'd thought. Good enough that I've earned a break. Have some fun, maybe, yes.

"'You taking the kid?'" Marty exits the Marine Parkway Bridge, heads down Flatbush Avenue.

"What?" Sarah asks.

"That's what Julius asked me. `You taking the kid?'"

"Does that mean me? I'm 'the kid'?" This delights her; she suspects it will continue to.

"Yeah." He bobs his head. "You're the kid."

"I like that."

He shrugs. "Whatever."

"I'm too old for Julius," Sarah says. Marty smiles slightly at her—he only ever smiles slightly at her—and adjusts the collar of his brown leather jacket. She wonders if he gets the joke, that Julius is fifty-eight, and she is therefore almost twenty-five years younger, but that this is still too old. That Marty, too, is fifty-eight, and so it is meant both as a joke and as a provocation. "You know, right?" she continues, to make sure. "You know I'm thirty-four?"

"Yeah, I know," says Marty, looking back at the road. "But I can't do anything about that."

———

HE HAS BEEN taking her places for over a month now: more shabbes evenings at Itzak's, where Darlene serves margaritas and he and Itzak reminisce about acid trips from the late sixties; day trips into Manhattan and a boat tour to the Statue of Liberty and Ellis Island; recording and editing sessions for two movies he's scoring at tiny studios in Williamsburg, where he ignored her for hours at a stretch while she tucked herself in a corner among abandoned coffee mugs propped on speakers, read *The Village Voice* and told herself she was doing research, like her shell book and walks on the beach, deepening her vision, gathering experience. Gathering layers, yes, allowing herself time. There is still plenty of time. He has taken her to dinner at a kosher Chinese restaurant, and to a vegetarian Israeli cafe. He insisted on buying her a new, unspattered color wheel and a seventy-five-dollar Isabey sable brush from an art supply shop in Park Slope, which, feeling guilty about her little shell painting waiting for her back in her room, she had reluctantly accepted. Saturday afternoons they have promenaded back and forth along the Rockaway Boardwalk, without bumping into each other, with their own separate bottles of water. When he runs into guys he knows from shul he leaves her standing to one side, shifting from foot to foot, while they talk. He likes to drive around Brooklyn neighborhoods and show her Orthodox Jews, the old men with sidelocks and tall hats trimmed with black fur, the heavily clothed women carrying stringed parcels and flocked by children in lisle knee socks. They fascinate him; he slows the car to a crawl, his hands splayed on the steering wheel, his mouth open, as if they're driving through a wildlife animal park.

What am I *doing* here? she sometimes says aloud to Marty. Who *is* this guy? she says, rhetorically, meaning him. This always gets one of his slight, amused smiles; she spaces saying this out carefully, to keep him amused.

She went to watch him play handball with his friend Saul, who is battling melanoma and whose thick, mascara'd-looking eyelashes appear bold and hale against his chemo'd scalp. She was the only woman, only girl, on the crowded playground in Riis Park; they were all men in their fifties and sixties, thwacking rubber balls hard and low around the court, breathing in rasps, sweating, all wearing gloves of thin leather with tiny holes like those in old men's fancy shoes. She sat on a bench and watched. A few times, when she caught Marty watching her watch, she held out her thumb like artists did once upon a time, squinting, tongue at the corner of her mouth, pretending to paint, to measure him in scale against the world; he posed for her in a position of mid-*thwack* and the guys, winded, gave him little shoves, knocking him out of the composition.

She wondered who or what they think she is to him. A niece, the daughter of a friend?

When one of them missed a ball and swore the others poked him, and jerked their heads at her. She was joined on the bench by a guy named Albie, who wasn't allowed to play; he showed her the inch-long scar on his thigh from a recent angioplasty and the Aztec-design pillbox in the left pocket of his shorts where he kept his nitroglycerin pills. No problem, she reassured him; her father keeps handy a bottle of those same infinitesimal white chips, she knows about angina and putting one under the tongue. She remembered coming home from eighth grade and finding her father gray, lying on the bathroom floor, rigid and limp with pain, her mother stumbling, rummaging in cabinets and drawers and babbling, *Sarah, thank God you're here, do something, do something!*

She'd told her mother to calm down, call 911, and she'd tipped her father's head back, dropped in the pill, assured and cradled him until the paramedics arrived.

She told Albie about her father's prostate cancer, that the hormone therapy and radiation seem to be working, that he's still able to play a lot of golf. Albie told her about a prostate piece in the *Times*, quoted statistics on morbidity and aging, then mournfully watched the other guys play. Marty gave her a clownish grin, waved, and went back to the game.

Once, walking down a block of musicians and street vendors and coffee houses in Greenwich Village, he stopped in front of a post-waif girl with chromate yellow glasses, on her knees, flipping through a slanted stack of weathered record albums.

"Oh, wow," he said to Sarah. "You're not going to believe this."

He leaned over the girl and pulled an album out; the cover was an overexposed black-and-white photo of a young man with wild, curly dark hair, handsome, bare-chested and somber, his eyes soulful, leaning against a big tree. He handed the album to Sarah and tapped the upper right corner: MARTY ZALE.

"This is *you*?" she asked.

"Yeah," he said, sheepish but pleased. "My Jim Croce era. Wow. This thing is over thirty years old."

"Are you going to buy it?"

"I've *got* it," he said. "I got it at home, I'll show you. I'll play it for you. The sound quality, it's different. You probably never heard the real thing." The album's cardboard shine was mottled, its corner tips worn gray and furred. He read the liner notes, nodding.

She was nonplussed by the old, young, exposed image of him. "It's sort of a relief," she said finally. He looked at her quizzically. "It's proof you are who you say you are," she said.

"Yeah." Then he regarded her a moment, baffled. "Aren't *you*?"

"SO, WAIT, ARE you sleeping with him?" her friend Emily asked on the phone.

"No. I don't even peck him good night on the cheek. He's never once touched me." She felt vaguely embarrassed, not knowing how to explain this . . . relationship? She doesn't even know what to call it. "Which is totally fine, by the way. My head isn't even in that space. I'm completely focused on work. That's the whole reason I'm here."

"I hope you're getting out to the beach, at least. The kids love it when we visit Nana."

"I was going for a lot of walks, at first. But it's so crowded now." Invaded, she didn't say, taken over by trespassing kids, and families with kids, kicking gritty sand on her oiled legs, leaving spittled pistachio shells and popsicle sticks and soda cans trickling out to dark blotches in the sand. Even the oyster and clamshells are gone; a tractor plows across the beach every morning, roaring into her bedroom window at six or seven AM, crushing everything down to smooth out the sand for feet and blankets and castles. The few unbroken shells left are quickly snatched up to make mermaid jewelry, to decorate battlements or pave moats. She is irritated by the simultaneous littering and scavenging of her beach by children and their silly sense of treasure. Their screeching. A walk on the beach now means dodging screaming kids with slopping bucketfuls of sea water, boomboxes turned up too loud and people screaming over summer pop tunes. Now, when she isn't out somewhere with Marty, she mostly stays inside or on Nana's porch, frustrated and annoyed that she is arranging her time this way. Like a still life with too central a focal point, with no sense of movement.

"Well, you have to. You have to go in swimming, at some point," Emily said.

"I will. I just haven't yet. I've been so busy. And the water's probably still pretty cold." Sarah heard children screaming in the background, suspicious crashing sounds. "What's going on?"

"The kids are dismantling the living room. I told them we need to clear space for the birthing tub. Hey, Rachel? Sweetie, don't let Elijah chew on that, okay? It's icky."

Sarah envisioned Emily's two howling kids, Rachel at three and Elijah at fourteen months, running amok in Emily's renovated eighteenth-century farmhouse, their cupid faces smeared with fresh-picked blueberries, wearing the tie-dye shirts and whimsical fairy wings made at neighbor children's birthday parties, spilling apple juice and climbing on the Stickley furniture. She pictured Emily, seven months pregnant, varicose, trodding around after them. The thought creeped her, gave her a headache. She and Emily are one month apart in age, and used to get their periods in sync.

"Sorry," Emily said in her ear. "We just had the sheep shorn, and Elijah likes chewing on the fleece. There's bags of it by the door, I haven't had time to get it washed and carded yet."

"'Baa baa black sheep, have you any wool?'"

"Don't, please. Rachel won't stop with that. I love my child, but I hear that one more time, I will have to kill her."

"How are you feeling?"

"Tired. Fecund. My parents are coming for the birth, and my Aunt Rose and Susan are bringing Nana, did I tell you?"

"How's she doing?"

"Amazing. Doing all her physical therapy and zipping around with her walker. She said there's no way she's missing it. And I really, really, want you to get here early and be my doula this time, all right? You should come maybe the first week of August."

"I'm there. I can't wait. I miss you."

"I miss you, too. And maybe you can do some work while you're here. If you can find a quiet and uncluttered spot."

"Yeah, maybe. So, are you squatting? Are you doing your perineal massage?"

"Yup. And Michael oils my labia every night. This is my life."

"That's why this is wonderful. I can experience the whole gruesome miracle through you, and not ever have to do it myself."

"You're welcome. Next baby, I'm hiring a surrogate." She heard Emily sigh. "Then I can run off and hang out with you somewhere. Frolic in the ocean."

"There aren't any sharks in the water around here, right?"

"I don't think so, that far north."

"What about jellyfish?"

"They're no big deal."

"Riptides?"

"Oh my God, listen to you. Don't worry, they put up a red flag if it's dangerous. Elijah, honey, come here. You want some nunu?" Sarah heard snaps, the fumbling with a strap.

"You still have milk?" Sarah asked.

"A little. It's more a comfort thing for him. And every time I nurse, I do Kegels."

"You're going to have vaginal walls of steel."

"Wonderful. Hey, are you still into that guy?"

"What guy?" She was startled, for a moment, thinking of Marty.

"That young guy you were dating. The kid. Dean?"

"David. Did my saying 'vaginal walls of steel' make you think of him?"

"I did vicariously enjoy those stories of yours."

"That's all over, sorry. We ended it when I left."

"Well, maybe the timing was off."

"Nah. It was just a fling."

"So, the big question, now."

"Yeah, yeah."

"You ready?"

"Go ahead."

"Are you painting?"

"Yes, of course. I mean, I *started* a painting," Sarah said. She glanced at the barely-begun canvas on her easel, at all the other canvases leaning against the walls of her room, still empty and inscrutable. "I started," she repeated. She lifted her new Isabey brush, inspected to see if it was fully clean, fully dry. "But it's just sitting there. It's barely a start, really. Maybe it's nothing."

This is flat, Sarah, her professor used to say. *Look at the flaw in your composition. The lack of perspective. You need to work on the illusion of depth!*

"Well, you just turned your life completely upside down for this. That can be pretty paralyzing. And there's a lot at stake. But look, you've started! That's the hardest part. Diving in."

"I know." She set her brush down. "I have hope. I'm keeping the faith."

"I can't wait to see it. I'm so really really glad you're doing this, finally."

"Me, too."

"It's what you're supposed to be doing."

"Well, thanks."

"It doesn't have to be perfect, you know. You always do that to yourself.

"I know."

"Just keep going."

"I will. I am. Okay?" She hears the edge in her voice, adds a casual chuckle.

"I don't mean to lecture you, I swear. I know I've got zero credibility. I haven't written a poem in six years."

"You've been busy. You're busy doing the most important thing in the world."

"Yeah, right."

"And you do it so well," Sarah said. "Really." Because everything you do, she thought, you do so well. Everything Emily does is important. Is interesting. She published two books of poetry before she was twenty-eight, she won prizes, scholarships, grants, she traveled, she married a rich and handsome man who gave her those exquisite, obnoxious children with her perfect curls and his solemn, Dutch master face. She makes fennel soup and knows what to do with monkfish, knows how to make chunks of tofu taste like heavy cream. At Halloween she carves Picasso and Modigliani pumpkins. She has done so much, already, effortlessly and perfectly and ahead of schedule. Her life is in Golden Section proportion. Sarah could hear Elijah sucking, gulping, pictured him draped across Emily's lap, and suddenly thought of that crazed guy taking a sledgehammer to the Pietà in Rome, the lunatic who'd gotten past Vatican security and smashed away at Mary's serene marble head, at Jesus's death-limp face.

"Rachel's been painting a lot," Emily was saying. "Of course, I think she's a genius. Maybe she takes after you."

"Ah. You mean she *isn't* painting a lot."

"Oh, Sarah. Maybe that's really what you're doing with that Marty guy."

"What?"

"Not painting."

"What if I just really don't *want* to paint?"

"Come on."

"Maybe that's what this summer is really about. Maybe painting *isn't* what I'm supposed to be doing. Maybe there's some whole other thing I just haven't figured out yet." She sat on the edge of her bed, feeling a little breathless.

"Like what?"

"Oh, I don't know . . . " She flopped back on the bed, considered the ceiling. She reached, brushed away the annoying grains of sand tucked between her toes. "Never mind. I'm just cranky. I'm just tired. Hey, maybe I can hire a surrogate painter."

"It's just . . . "

"What?"

"You always find something, you know? Some excuse."

"What does that mean?"

"Well, like grad school. Chicago."

She sat up. "That wasn't a choice, Em. My dad had to have the bypass. I had to go home."

"Exactly. *Go* home. That's what it sounded like then, when you told me. Not *move* home. Not *stay* home. Then he got through it just completely fine and next thing you're telling me you got an apartment there, about the art store job, you're all settled in. And I'm thinking, 'Wait, what about Chicago?'"

"Because then my mom rear-ended that guy, and my dad still couldn't drive for months afterward. They needed help."

"They could have hired someone."

"They couldn't afford that. Not everybody can afford that, Em." She hears her edge again, tries to soften her tone. "They aren't hire-help people."

"You could've gone the next year. You could have. The Institute was going to hold your scholarship."

She climbed off the bed. She paced.

"Sarah?"

She approached her easel, studied her shell painting.

"They really wanted you," Emily continued. "You chose not to go."

A tiny sable hair was stuck in a stroke of black paint, like a wandering eyelash.

"I just worry about you. You've been doing this for-ever. Being so responsible for them. Trying to make up for Aaron. I get worried, I worry you've allowed them to—"

"You know, Emily," and she was aware of the brusque tone again, the hard-hitting *Em*, but didn't care, "I've been sort of busy, too, you know? I have a lot of stuff to deal with."

"I know. I didn't—"

"Maybe it's not like having a bunch of kids and sheep running around and a big Martha Stewart estate to look af-ter and which organic herbs to grow. But they're my *parents*, you know? I'm their daughter. And you're right, I'm all they have left. So, what do you want me to do, abandon them in some old age home? Warehouse them, so I can go play?"

"That's not what I'm saying. I'm not talking about logistics."

"This is real life stuff. Real life problems. It's probably hard for you to understand, when you get total freedom to make all these great *choices*."

There was silence, then a faint, milky baby gasp, then silence again.

"I'm sorry, Em. Really. That was obnoxious. That was my envious evil twin inner-demon talking."

"It's okay."

"I get your point, really. They make me crazy. And I let them. I'm three thousand miles away, and I still totally buy into it."

"I know. I'm sorry."

"It's like . . . " She started pacing again. "It's like, I called them the other day, and they really have been supportive, you know, they actually haven't called even *once* I've been here, and so each day they don't call I feel even more incredibly guilty. So I call to see how they are, and they ask how much work I'm getting done. Which sounds nice, but what they really mean is, I'm *supposed* to be getting all this *interesting recent* work done, because that's why I'm here and not there, right? This big exhibit, this once-in-a-lifetime opportunity. This very *legitimate* reason for abandoning them. And I don't even answer, because then they're telling me my dad can't program the VCR or the sprinkler system and he can't find his pills and where do I get those low-fat muffins he can eat, and my mom can't drive at all after the last DUI, and the doctor's threatening to take her off the transplant list if she doesn't quit drinking, and then they bicker and my mom gets weepy and my dad gets pissed off and they say how much they miss me and love me, how proud they are, and how I am the most wonderful daughter in the world. And when am I coming home? And then we all hang up and I feel crazy. Just totally crazy." She took a breath, forced another little chuckle.

There was another silence, then:

"You know, Sarah," and she could hear Emily choosing, saying her words very carefully, "taking care of your parents, and doing every little thing for them exactly the way they would like it done, are two different things."

"I know that."

"You *do* take good care of them. You always will. You will always be sure they are warm and safe and comfortable, right?"

"Of course. But that's not—"

"You haven't abandoned them. You *are* a good daughter."

"Thanks. I guess, sure. But—"

"But they're not happy people, Sarah. You can't make them into happy people. There isn't enough of you in the world to do that."

There was a faint, fun-filled shriek, a sudden amped-up

up blare of pop music. She looked out the open picture window, peered down at the beach. Kids were chasing each other across the sand, screeching and swinging strips of seaweed. A vendor was hawking ice-cold soft drinks from a wheeled cooler. Teenage girls rubbing suntan lotion on each other, mock-squealing, teenage boys zigzagging with surfboards, or kicking around a soccer ball, *thwack thwack thwack*. No wonder she was feeling a headache, that dull burn looming at her temples, behind her eyes. She swung shut the window, twisted the latch tight.

"You're not crazy," Emily was saying. "But forget 'supposed to.' Don't even paint, if you don't want to. You deserve to just have some complete fun and be totally silly and footloose and irresponsible for now. You really do."

"Maybe."

"You know the real truth? I wish I could be doing all that. What you're doing right now." Through the phone Sarah heard a girl child wail, scream *Mommy! Mommy!* She heard a man's voice, *Emily? Honey, can you come here . . . ?* and another Emily sigh in her ear. "There you go. Truth is, I am consumed with envy. I hate you."

"Thank you. That's better."

"I can't wait to see you."

"Me too. Thanks. I'm sorry about before."

"Oh, please. I love you."

"I love you, too."

"Hey, did I tell you we have ducklings now? And we're going to start keeping bees."

"You are out of your mind. You are the crazy one."

"I know. So please, go have some sexy beach-bum fun, for me. Go splash around in the ocean. Go have a meaningless hot fling with that musician. Go play. Report back. I'll be here."

———

THE SATELLITES, THE guys they pick up for the ride to the gig, all in turn exit brick and stone and ivy-covered houses in placid, graceful Brooklyn neighborhoods. They are guys she hasn't met: Tony, Frankie, Sammy, cramming in the back of Marty's silver BMW, wearing their black suits and fedoras and Ray Bans. This is Sarah, Marty says to each, she's coming with. They nod and wink at her as they wedge their way in, then burst into loud buddy-jostling. Hey, Rabbi, Tony yells to Marty, what was the name of that asshole in Atlantic City, that time we opened for Leno? Tell it to the Rabbi, Frankie says to Tony, he's gonna love this, Hey Rabbi, get off at the BQE, Rabbi lemme sing the lead on that one, huh?

They are all Italian, and sound to her like supporting characters from a Scorsese movie. Like most of Marty's friends—besides Julius, who is a stockbroker—none of them seem to work, to have jobs. Frankie complains about a flood in his basement garage threatening his Alfa Romeo. Tony spends weeks out on his houseboat. Sammy plays a lot of bridge. They all have state of the art gadgets, expensive shoes, nails manicured to a dull, opalescent shine. She is convinced they are all, peripherally, Mafia. *Goodfellas*, exactly. Each of them apparently has had one or two brushes with the music industry: Frankie wrote a hit song in the sixties; Sammy played keyboard on a double album that went platinum; Tony produced one blockbuster tour in the early seventies. She is leery of this day, of this event, nervous of these guys dressed up for their gig in their pitched fedoras and slick, raven-black suits. Their energy is slightly ridiculous, like teenage boys hyped and anxious about their garage band, but the trinkets—the fancy cars and gold watches and quietly costly homes—are reassuring to her: they have something else. Something real. She is disappointed in herself to feel this way, just as she was ashamed at her relief when she finally saw Marty's house for the first time, not the small brick one she'd thought was his, a better one, beachfront, expansive, probably worth several million, and thought Good, he's not just some weirdly religious, aging musician bum. She has found herself liking how he smells, but was abashed when she realized it was partly the BMW scent, a fresh leather-and-citrus, air-conditioned tang, a whiff of rich oil. The whole idea of the gig today is ridiculous to her, an Oldies celebration, oh God. She is worried he will look ridiculous, like Bowser from that old Sha Na Na group, or the aging actors in *Grease*, pathetic and earnestly anachronistic, that there will be slicked-back, thinning hair and silly dance moves. It all seems childish. Better he be a thoroughly grown-up man, established and defined by something else, something maybe artistic but still secure and status'd, like scoring films.

Before they leave Sammy's house, the last stop, Marty asks her if she wants to go to the bathroom. It's a long drive. He smiles encouragingly, and she almost expects him to pat her on the head. When she gets back in the car they're all humming together, testing sound. Tony clears his throat with a loud hack, and Sammy blows his nose. For the first half hour on the road, as they leave the urban and suburban sprawl and head north on the 95 through sweet bedroom communities and increasingly lush countryside along Long Island Sound, Frankie tries teaching her about music. He talks about chords and modulation and the principles of harmonics, No, Rabbi, lemme explain it to her, see, an octave, that's really thirteen tones but the diatonic scale, Western harmony's all based on that, it only uses eight of those, that's our do re mi, look at piano keys, eight white, five black, now those are semi-tones, half-steps . . . But it snarls up in her head like math, like junior-high equations on the chalkboard. She tries to nod politely at what he is saying, but the truth is, she doesn't really listen, she doesn't really care.

"WELCOME TO RYE, PLAYLAND! HOST OF WCBS 101.1 FM, NEW YORK'S SALUTE TO THE OLDIES!" comes in amplified static over the loudspeaker, barely audible over parkgoers screaming, laughing, calling, the hawking at carnival-style win-the-teddy bear games, and the tinny circus music piped from Playland attractions: Skyflier, The Derby Racer, Aladino's Flying Carpet! Marty and the guys are unloading equipment, looking around for the other two Satellites meeting them here. Technicians in sweat-damp "Playland Hosts 101.1 FM's Salute to the Oldies" T-shirts bolt around wearing headsets and carrying fistfuls of cable wire, dragging bleachers together. Sarah stretches, and wonders if there's food. She hopes there's something to drink. Everyone is sweating in the sun.

"WE HAVE BEN E. KING, THE DRIFTERS, THE HARPTONES, MARTY ZALE & THE SATELLITES! LIVE PERFORMANCE AND BROADCAST, BEGINS 7:30 ON THE MAIN STAGE!"

The Cyclone, the Dragon Coaster, the Gondola Wheel! The air smells of corn kernels bursting in hot salted oil, and sugar melted brown and thick to caramel. Food stands sell Carvel's Ice Cream and Hebrew National foot-long hot dogs. A fried dough concession offers three toppings: powdered sugar & cinnamon, tomato sauce with cheese, and strawberry jelly. There is a photography booth with garish Gay Nineties costumes, a Haunted Mansion Thrills 'n Chills edifice blasting witchy, shrieking laughter, and, Sarah notes thankfully, kiosks selling sixteen-ounce paper cups of beer—Miller Lite and Bud, on tap. Kids, everywhere. It's as bad as the beach in Rockaway, children swarming, grubby and hyperkinetic. They bump their faces against sticky, shiny pillows of cotton candy, dart away from the beery or sugared-up adults clutching empty sixteen-ounce cups in one hand and grabbing at the backs of their kids' T-shirts with the other. Like all those kiddie parties in loud, family-frenzy places like this, the whimsical silly childhood birthdays at amusement parks, Miss Genie's Wonderland, Swenson's, Farrell's Olde Fashioned Ice Cream Parlour. Bright whole family days, her parents, her baby brother, days rooted in gladness and giddy surprise, hugs and presents and laughing, sticky tabletops, gleeful screaming friends wearing balloon-twist hats, *Happy Birthday, dear Sarah, Happy Birthday To You!!*

"So," she says to Marty, feeling a little dazed. "Playland, huh?"

"Wait here," he says. "I have to go get set up backstage, then we'll walk around together. You okay? You cold? You want my jacket?"

"It's ninety degrees."

"It's going to get cold, later."

"I'm fine," she tells him. "Look, I've got long sleeves. I'm just . . . out of context here. Go ahead."

"So, you wait here, right?"

"I'll walk around a little. I'll come back."

"Well . . . yeah, okay. Don't get lost. Wait, you need some money?"

"Uh, no," she says, blinking, smiling. "I'm fine."

"All right. So later we'll play a game, or go the Ferris wheel, or something. We'll get ice cream."

"That all may be a little too whimsical for me." She has the sudden hideous image of his trying to win her a stuffed panda, but smiles at his hopeful face.

"Yo, Zale!" Tony is standing with a perspiring, grinning man wearing a battered 101.1 FM baseball cap, carrying a clipboard; both men wave frantically at Marty.

He waves back. "That's Russell, the DJ. I have to go see about stuff now." He hurries off in a rapid amble, a tall guy hunched at the shoulders, his curly hair flapping out from under the fedora.

Marty Zale & the Satellites.

Who is this guy? she thinks. What am I doing here?

MARTY FINDS HER an hour later sitting on a bench near the whirling Gondola wheel, eating a foot-long and drinking a Diet Coke; she had really wanted a Miller Lite, but it is only four-thirty in the afternoon and she doesn't want him to see her drinking so early.

"What are you doing?" he asks. "What is that?"

"A hot dog. I was starving."

"How can you eat that?" He looks disapproving. "It's *treyf*."

"All right. What's 'treyf'?"

"Impure. Filthy."

"I thought that was *hazerai*."

"Well . . . it's unkosher, then."

"It is not. It's Hebrew National." She waves the wrapper at him.

He shudders at her, and takes a seat on the bench. "I'll take you out for dinner later, afterward." He scans the crowd, his eyes narrowing behind the dark glasses. "This is good, right? Yeah? All the families out with kids." He chews his lip.

"Yeah. Are you nervous?"

"No, not really." He looks at the jagged current of people. "Wow. Look at them." A couple in their mid-seventies stroll by, dressed in matching Playland T-shirts wrinkled up over their stomachs and holding hands with a deliberate, tender consciousness. "That's sweet."

"Probably married sixty years," Sarah says.

"Yeah. Three dozen great-grandkids. Still coming to Playland. Holding hands. Hey, there, look." He points out a cluster of pre-teenish girls, roaming. Their braces flash, they giggle and grab at each other and swing their hair, their eyes darting around, watching, always looking. The ritual. Sarah remembers being one of them, a roaming, watching girl. She knows they smell like mint or cinnamon gum, and sweetish drugstore cosmetics, and the faint bitter beginnings of women's sweat. She remembers having that snug, fluid skin. Perfect skin. You don't appreciate it at the time, being dewy, you're too inside of it to see. Flesh that both absorbs and gives off the light. And so hard to paint, to capture that, to pin that kind of living skin to canvas.

"Which one were you?" Marty asks.

"Hmm?"

"Which of them were you? Look, that one's the leader, right?" The one who looks fourteen but isn't yet, leggy, wearing a sixteen-year-old's halter top and miniskirt, who knows not to blow-dry her curly blonde hair but to let it swirl, who knows what they're roaming and watching for. "She isn't the oldest, but she gets it, she knows what's going on."

"Yeah," Sarah says.

"Then that one, with the baby fat, she's older, but she's scared. She's scared of the blonde, but she wants that, to be like that. She's thirteen, fourteen, but she's really ten. The little one there, she's sweet, just a kid, but she's modest, you know? How she's dressed. That's nice. Like how you dress, the long skirts and sleeves. *Tzenius*, that means modest."

"I don't know if I was any of them. I don't remember being that young," says Sarah.

"Yeah, you're so old now."

"See? I told you. My youth is gone. It's over. No more whimsy."

"You're like a little girl, still. You'll get married, have kids . . . "

"No kids."

"What do you mean, no kids? You got to have kids."

"No, I don't. I don't want any. I've never wanted to have kids."

"Why?"

"I'm . . . just not into it. Way too much responsibility."

"Huh."

"It's really okay," she says with a laugh.

"There's that saying that adults think they make babies, but it's really babies that make adults."

"Not always. Not necessarily." She finishes her Diet Coke, and tosses the cup in a trashcan near the bench. "And are you saying I have to have a baby in order to be an adult?"

"No. But it's an important way."

"I agree. But there's other ways." She watches him chew at his lip again. He hums. "What's wrong?"

"Nothing. You know, whatever. Come on, let's walk."

"You look . . . I don't know. Not happy."

"I'm happy."

"You're not nervous about the show?"

"No, I love this, I love doing this. That's why I'm here. Me and the guys, we've been doing this twenty years now. Russell, the DJ, you know, for the radio station? We go back twenty-five, thirty years."

"Something's wrong."

"Yeah, well . . . " He peers at her, and she decides he's happy with her, that he thinks she's perceptive. She smiles a little, trying to look sensitive and understanding. "So, sure, I feel funny," he says. "It's Saturday. I feel guilty being here."

"Oh." She gets it. "Because it's shabbes." He nods. "But this isn't work. It's not like Julius, off manipulating capital. Committing usury. You're not defiling the Temple."

"Maybe this's worse. More self-indulgent, maybe. Like I'm just playing around, not being serious about it."

"Like you're not honoring God?"

He hesitates, then nods again, slowly. "I don't know, God, I don't know if there even *is* a God, but yeah, what you mean by that. Whatever."

"You don't believe in God? How can a religious fanatic not believe in God?"

"I'm not a fanatic. You think I'm a fanatic?"

"No. I'm just trying to provoke you."

"You are?" He seems glad. "That's good. Okay. Look, it's about that consciousness, you know? It isn't just—"

"Blind adherence to an irrational and sexist belief system."

"Right, yeah. It's about a spiritual consciousness. The laws, the customs, that's all bullshit, you know? That's all *religion*. I don't study Torah to just memorize that stuff, I'm talking about what they call *religiosity*, that's the longing, see, the real creative longing. Awareness. You want to hook into this mystery, this thing at the core of it all, in everything you do. You have to create it with every single act. Maybe that's communion, God, I don't know. You got to search for it in every act you do, every decision. Every choice. You know what sin is, real sin? Inertia. Refusing to act. Refusing the responsibility for your own life."

"Right." She feels at a loss. "Okay, I get it."

"In the Baal Shem it says 'the God of Abraham, God of Isaac, God of Jacob.' We don't say 'the God of Abraham, Isaac, and Jacob,' right? Because each one of us has to search for it. Our own sense of the divine. Of God. By *doing*. Being in the world. You see what I mean?"

No, she doesn't, not quite. She wonders if he is judging her. She feels unspiritual, heathen, in danger of seeming disrespectful. But hasn't she always tried to make the good and thoughtful decisions, the right choices? Hasn't she always been so responsible about everything?

"Hey, man, excuse me, you're Marty Zale, huh?" A guy in his mid-twenties, carrying an enormous acrylic sheepdog won at some carnival game, creeps up to them, stands with nervous, elastic knees.

"Yeah," says Marty, smiling.

"Oh, shit, man." The guy clutches the sheepdog by its ears and sets it down, revealing a *Marty Zale & The Satellites* T-shirt. He grabs Marty's hand for shaking. "I've seen you guys everywhere, you know, Atlantic City and that place in Philly, I came to Boston once, I'm always keeping an eye out for you, you know?" He glances at Sarah. "Hey, excuse me."

"No problem," she says. She pictures this poor bouncing guy wandering the East Coast in a Greyhound bus, hitching rides, saving ticket stubs for scrapbooking, buying T-shirts.

"Thanks," Marty says.

"Shit, man, you guys are the *best*. You're real, I'm serious, you're *actual*."

"That's really nice. That's great," says Marty.

"Yeah, I'll catch you guys later, huh? I mean, I'm there, later, front row."

"Beautiful," says Marty. "Thanks."

"No, hey, *me* thanks. Excuse me, huh?" The guy backs up with his sheepdog, gives them an enthused thumbs-up, and springs off.

Sarah chuckles at Marty's pleased face. "You look tickled," she says.

"It isn't about that," he says. "It isn't."

"I know." It won't necessarily be horrible, she thinks. He can't be too bad.

"I mean, that's nice, okay, right, but that's the bullshit part, too."

"That kid is bullshit?"

"No, no, I mean, if we're connected that way, me and that kid, that's beautiful. If the *music* did that."

"I know," she repeats. "The music's what counts."

"Yeah. That's . . . here." He puts his hand on his chest. "The applause stuff? That's out there."

"Well," she says, "you could say it would be dishonest or dishonorable or just stupid blind adherence to rules to deny that inside part of you. The music part. Maybe not doing music would be the sin. Maybe by doing that, by honoring that, you *are* honoring God. Maybe *that* is your conscious communion." Sinatra was dignified, right? "Really. Don't worry. The angels will bless you."

"Hmm." He regards her thoughtfully, and slowly smiles. "What?"

"I always feel better with you," he says. "Why is that?"

She has no idea, but she suddenly feels a bright happiness at his inclusive *with you*. She looks away from him, confused. She doesn't want to be included in him.

"So . . . " she says to the space in front of her. "You want to walk around for a while?" She looks back over her shoulder; he is in the middle of reaching out to her with one hand, the hand he'd put to his heart. She's noticed his hands before, on the steering wheel, pouring wine at Itzak's, shaping her an oyster. They're beautiful. They're young hands, like her father's hands are still a young man's hands, fresh-skinned, steady, expressive. David had beautiful hands, too, she thinks, but he was only twenty-four. His hands looked younger than hers. He needed to be with someone with twenty-two-year-old hands, veinless, tendonless. Perfect skin on a perfect girl, not some horrible woman who's messed up, who's messed herself up. She can't remember if David felt that way, or she felt that way. This hand, Marty's hand, looks to be headed toward her, as if to caress her hair, but doesn't—this hand hovers in the air a moment, suspended, then drops to his side.

They look at each other, then she rises to her feet and forces out a twirl for him, just one, a silly, hopeful twirl. His face brightens, almost into a laugh. He at once appears inordinately delighted with her, and uses her proffered arm to pull himself up.

HE INSISTS ON leaving her his brown leather jacket this time. He leaves her to go do the sound check, warm up with the guys, get focused, whatever. A few hundred people have gathered around the main stage, but the crowd has shifted older in age; they're people in their forties and fifties and sixties eager for the Oldies they remember from when they weren't. Only a few whole families are left, parents holding slack, dangling toddlers. Sarah checks his jacket pockets: keys, a wallet without any photos, and a foiled, half-eaten roll of Rolaids.

"LADIES AND GENTLEMEN, LET'S GIVE IT UP FOR . . . THE DRIFTERS!"

There is applause and cheers, and a start-up doo-wop bounce of music for the old guys gripped in blue shark-skin suits running out on stage. Sarah decides it's time for a drink. She swallows the first Miller Lite quickly, dawdling near the beer kiosk, then buys another and strolls with it, keeping fifty or sixty yards away from the stage so the music pleasantly mutes. The sun is slipping, and tiny white lights are flickering on everywhere, like the fireflies blinking bright in the fields around Emily's house in Connecticut. The day's heat is slipping away, too, and wisps of cotton candy float by on the final warm drifts of air. She loves this exact moment, when the summer night coolness lifts and crisps and the color values darken, first toned with grays then shaded with blacks, until the colors themselves are absorbed away.

When the first blush of alcohol in her blood alchemizes every pulse. When cotton candy floats like seraphim and she senses herself delicate, fine-boned, full of a holy glow. Every instant feels rich, as if everything is fine, as if something could still happen. Maybe. She takes another sip.

She notices the group of adolescent girls nearby, the ones she noticed earlier in the day, gathered in a small, brightly-lit booth: "Body Art by Art—Temporary Tattoos by Design." Two of them, giggling, have bared their midriff and shoulder for smeary transfers of a budding red rose and an ovoid yin and yang. The little one—the modest one, Sarah recalls, *tzenius*—stands to one side, hugging herself, just watching. Every few minutes the girl glances longingly at the booth behind her friends, where for three scrim tickets and three well-aimed throws of a ping pong ball you could win a stuffed knock-off Snoopy or a Garfield with bulging plastic eyes. The blonde girl in the halter top has her coltish naked legs propped on a table, her slim right ankle offered up for an intricate Celtic-design cuff in faux India ink. The tattooer—Art?—is a Latino guy in his twenties, who looks bored by the girls but absorbed in his work. The Celtic anklet takes a long time. A bunch of sparsely stubbled teenage boys linger nearby, kicking the ground, flexing, scrutinizing, and the girls getting marked scrutinize back.

"LADIES AND GENTLEMEN, LET'S GIVE IT UP FOR
A GOOD BUDDY OF MINE, WE'RE LUCKY TO HAVE
'EM HERE, YOU ALL KNOW WHO I'M TALKING
'BOUT . . . MARTY ZALE & THE SATELLITES!"

She leans against a rear bleacher, sipping beer, wearing Marty's jacket draped over her left shoulder, feeling a
nervous twinge in her stomach. Maybe the hot dog, maybe it's just cramps, she thinks. Or the heat, all that noise,
the clapping.

Marty and the guys stroll out to loud cheery applause,
full of hoots and people waving like family members at a
wedding or birthday's end. The guy with the fuzzy acrylic
sheepdog jars her roughly as he pushes to the front; she
grips the waxy rim of her paper cup in her teeth so she can
clap, and moves back farther from the crowd. The applauding goes on. She clamps down harder on the cup's rim and
claps methodically. Clap clap clap. She knows she's at the
edge of being just drunk enough or not, holding on to the
rim of being drunk. Like mermaids and monkeys, she
thinks, pictures in her mind. Tiny plastic mermaid arms
and monkey tails in bright acid pinks and greens, holding on, hanging on to root beer floats, hooked on the rims
of glass mugs in places like this. Gaudy, celebratory, reek-
ing of sugar. Farrell's Ice Cream Parlour, *Don't you want a
party, Sarah?* her parents asked, insisted, *It's your birthday!*,
so determined to create celebration, give her a regular little

girl-ness, although she already feels herself too old for an ice cream parlor birthday. She is eleven.

But *Do it for your mother, Sarah,* her father says, *She needs this right now, do it for her,* and so of course she did, of course she does, give her mother her birthday, and it's a day spent holding her breath among her friends' ice-cream-drunk giggles and balloon-twist hats, waiting for the awful thing, her mother laughing too loudly too festive too grim, her father clapping his hands too hard with forced gaiety, clap clap clap. She sees her mother pouring vodka into her Tab from a purse-sized plastic bottle meant to hold Jean Naté body splash, she sees her father see it, sees her father's face tightening darkening, wait it's coming, yes, her mother's laughter turning slack and weepy, there it is, her mother's hands shaking as she carries in the bright-iced cake, everyone singing the inharmonious "Happy Birthday" too loud, ice cream parlor bells and whistles, her mother shaking, stumbling, the cake sliding, dropping to break and smash on the floor.

Gasps, wails, mock-clapping, awkward laughter. She sees her father tipping into the release of anger, grabbing her mother, his grip brutal on her arm, *Sarah, come help me, come here!,* but which of them even said that at that moment, which of them was pleading *Sarah, do something, come help,* demanding her to help clean it all up, to make everything all right? She won't do it, no, is looking down, away from her parents, her mortified friends, she is studying all those pink plastic mermaids hanging from glass mugs, the chartreuse monkeys hooked from their skinny plastic tails, and she hates her crying slumping mother, her raging father, hates candles and cakes, hates her little brother for dying, hates her pretty friend from school with the prettiest curly hair, Emily, hates her for her pretty look of pity and the well-packed nutritious lunches she brings to school. She hates herself for having a birthday. She grips a tiny acid-pink mermaid in her fist, feels a tiny plastic arm snap off like a wishbone, and, later that night, when the day is over with and done and cleaned up and never again please be forgotten forever, in the quiet of her bedroom she sits on her bed, presses the pink plastic bone edge of a mermaid arm against the skin of her thigh, deeper, feels the quick hot pierce, begins to carve *S*, then *AR*, *AH* into her flesh, each bleeding letter in happy bright red focus, she is here, yes, she is here, she is here.

A surge of applause startles her; she looks up to see Russell the DJ leap onstage to embrace Marty, and the two guys quip with each other, Yeah, we go back, huh?, I'll tell you folks, I knew this guy when . . . A perm'd, fleshy woman in her late forties begins yelling out requests. The sheepdog guy hoots. Marty and Tony and Frankie and Sammy laugh, bobbing their heads, waving, then Marty starts to sing, the other Satellites backing him on keyboard and bass, their voices in support of his. And Sarah blinks because she *sees* it, suddenly, sees the music of their voices like pure white light through a prism, split into all the colors of sound.

Harmony, she thinks, *oh*. I get it now. Marty sings the ruling color, intense, dominant, red purple, maybe, an ultramarine mixed with alizarin crimson, and Tony, Frankie, Sammy sing the complements, they're yellow orange, yellow green, blue green, the perfect meld to balance, texture, highlight each other, all the hues swirling together, the relationship of note to note, *that's* what music is, we should have been listening to *music* in all those art classes, trying to grasp color, refraction, translucence, perspective, the illusion of depth, and, okay, you know what, Sarah? You have had a *lot* to drink. No wonder this is so bearable.

She unbites the cup and breathes, tries to just listen and know the harmony is a stable, tangible thing. It isn't going to go away or suddenly clash, she can trust it, hold on. She breathes, peaceful and wildly relieved, watching music. The jacket over her left shoulder floats up a smell of oil-rich leather, and citrus with a touch of salt; she slides her arms into the sleeves and pulls it around her, warm as a sun-hot towel, a palm of coconut lotion. She tucks her nose in the collar, huddles like a crustacean. She resists the urge to wave at Marty, up above onstage.

"Having fun?" Russell the DJ is standing next to her.

"Oh, sure," she says. "This is completely great." I love these guys, she thinks. These old guys singing in their little black fedoras and shades are good, this is a completely charming thing. This is so sweet. She smiles happily at Russell. "I never heard them before this."

"No? Never?" he says, surprised.

Oh, right, she reminds herself. I'm the girl with the band. She laughs to herself; she has never, ever, this she knows, been the type of girl to be the girl with the band.

"Well, I'll tell you, they're the best, these guys. Never made the charts or anything, you know, but they're the real thing. Look at this crowd. They're all in love. I see some of these people all the time, they follow these guys around to every gig." His voice layers over the music like glaze.

"That's nice." She swallows what's left in her cup.

"And that one, he's my boy. Marty," Russell nods enthusiastically. "We go back a long time."

"So I've heard."

"Yeah, I'll tell you, you should've seen that one twenty years ago. Gorgeous."

"Really?" she says. "Him?" She wishes, suddenly, that she had bought the album of his they'd found that day on the street. She wishes she'd looked more closely at it.

"Sure. That wild hair, and the voice, and that face. Look at that face. He's beautiful."

She watches Marty a moment, trying to superimpose that older, younger image. No, he's just some shlubby old singing guy, she thinks. Who shoves the Torah at me and *davens* and eats green onion stalks like pretzel sticks and whom I can't figure any angle of, I can't fit into any frame. She watches him standing out in front of the others, singing, with his beautiful hands up, caressing the air, looking ardent and happy and full of light. Oh, no, she thinks. He is. He is really, really beautiful, and you're all caught up and ridiculous and hearing colors like some strung-out groupie, and now it is too late, something has started, has begun.

The sheepdog guy keeps hooting. She wonders if he's a normal, enthused fan, or beyond that. Beyond *actual*. If he's really deranged, unhinged, lost, and there's a shotgun sewn into the big stuffed dog, rounds of ammo tucked inside his commemorative *Marty Zale* T-shirt. If maybe he's just waiting for the perfect, musical, vulnerable moment to snap and start spraying, to turn on her, take her out, obliterate and make everything end right now. She can't decide which way she'd like it to go.

———

SHE WAITS FOR him in the car, still wearing his jacket, watching him finish up autographs for the lingering fans. He glances up, sees her, waves. She waves back. *Take your time*, she mouths. But he says his good-byes, bear-hugs Russell, and hurries over.

"So?" he says, climbing into the driver's seat next to her.

"So?" she asks, smiling. He glances at her a little too casually, as if to say her reaction warrants a polite inquiry but doesn't really matter all that much. "So, that was great," she says, laughing, nodding. "You guys were really great."

"That was good, right?"

"Yeah. I'm . . . I have to say, I'm surprised. It's another whole different side of you. Like a glimpse into your soul."

"Yeah?"

"I really enjoyed it."

"I didn't see you anywhere."

"I was way in back. Russell came over to say hi."

"Good, I asked him to take care of you."

They both gaze straight ahead; Tony, Sammy, and Frankie are still joking around with Russell.

"Do you still have to go finish up anything?" she asks.

"No, I'm okay. It's good to just sit a minute, you know, come down from it. Whatever. Be peaceful. We'll go to dinner now, with the guys. Maybe we'll go to Elaine's."

Be scared of me, she thinks. Go on. Be, just a little, terrified. "I sort of got you a present," she says after a moment.

"Yeah?" He smiles slightly at her.

"Yeah." She slides his jacket off her shoulders, and twists away from him, facing the passenger door. She tugs sideways at the V-neck of her shirt until her left shoulder slips up through the neckline, and turns her show of naked back toward him. "I wanted to do something whimsical."

She thinks she hears him smile, then turns to look and sees him laugh, a warm little laugh of delight. Low on her left shoulder blade is a faux India ink tattoo in Art's meticulous cursive script: *Marty Zale & The Satellites*, garnished with musical notes and a floating G clef.

"I like this," he says. He's very pleased.

"It isn't real," she says. "Just temporary."

"This is good. A side to you I haven't seen."

"Good," she says. "Then we're even." She turns back to look out the window again, leaving her shoulder bare. She feels even before he does it his hand reach out and his finger trace the tattoo, gliding slowly over the letters on her skin. Then down below the triangular slope of shoulder blade, the smooth, still-perfect skin of her shoulder blade, to first up then down the sides of her spine, then high across the nape of her neck, tracing her collarbone, her throat, places where the tattoo is not.

MITZVAH

SARAH FINDS THIRTY-two-ounce plastic bottles of aloe-vera and ginseng moisturizer with alpha-hydroxy acids on sale at the drugstore on 116th Street; she buys three of them, so that every night she can coat herself thickly in forgiving, rejuvenating lotion, let her dry skin drink it all in while she sleeps. She buys baby oil to smooth on in the shower, and a pumice stone to grate her elbows and heels—rubbery bits of epidermis on the tile floor—and a loofah for husking the backs of her thighs. A cleanser made of ground apricot seeds, for sloughing her face free of dead cells. Tiny ampoules of

pure Vitamin E, to puncture and squeeze the healing, erasing oil out of. She buys a new pack of razors, for keeping her
legs shaved to an infantile satin. She stands for ten minutes or
so contemplating the SPF in various sunscreens, and finally
chooses a 35—lax enough to maintain a healthy, youthful
glow, but still enough, she decides, to block out all the aging and cancerous rays. A white plastic trapezoid of Johnson
& Johnson dental floss; Rembrandt toothpaste with special
whiteners. She looks for white cotton gloves in the ladies ap-
parel shops to wear overnight on her lotioned hands, but can't
find any. At a fruit stand next to the Pickles and Pies Delicatessen she buys lemons to squeeze into her hair, the whiff of
them bringing a fading, lemony moment, her mother doing
that when she was a very little girl, squeezing and combing
fresh lemons into her hair, the juice dripping down her bare,
chicken-bone back, tossing the lemon rinds to grind up in
the sink's garbage disposal so the kitchen would smell fresh.
Then sending Sarah out to sun, or all of them heading off to
the beach. But her hair was bright then, anyway, the natural blond of little girls' blond hair, the kind that tones down,
fades, has faded over time to a mousy dun. She hopes the
lemons will bring all the brightness back.

DINNER AT ELAINE'S was not what she'd expected. Tony and Frankie came with them, hyped up from the Playland gig, drumming their thighs like bongos, springing in their chairs. All three of them still wearing their doo-wop suits, their black fedoras cocked at smug angles. Marty let his hand wander down her back as he guided her to the table, then ignored her once they were all seated. The guys audited every song of the Oldies show, every note, Rabbi, that was sweet, I'm telling you, that last song, what you did, beautiful man, Frankie, we gotta work on that chorus, Hey, you guys see Nathan in the audience, did he show, or what? They crooned to each other over their rigatoni—she couldn't decide if she was present enough for them to be serving as audience, or was simply the generic and negligible girl with the band.

The place was empty, harshly lit; she'd imagined the scene from *Manhattan*, Woody Allen and dewy Mariel Hemingway glowing in soft-filtered black and white, heads together, an intimate twosome amidst a glamorous throng.

Instead, Tony suggested new songs for their repertoire, Frankie argued, and Marty nodded, contemplating, serious and absorbed as a high court judge. No one spoke to her. She asked the waiter for another glass of wine, ate a twenty-two-dollar endive and goat cheese salad, hoped the ridiculous *Marty Zale & The Satellites* inked on her shoulder wasn't staining her shirt. Tony announced he wanted to go back to Marty's that night, right then, work on that one bit—Rabbi, I'm telling you, you gotta hear it with the music—while it was still fresh. Frankie argued, and Marty decided Yeah, they should. He inquired if Sarah didn't really want dessert, did she? Tony and Frankie were already tensed to go, the balls of their feet scraping the floor, and Marty was gripping the arms of his chair; just to punish all of them, to insist on her presence in the room, she ordered a chocolate soufflé. It took forty-seven doo-wopping, table-tapping, jostling minutes to arrive and she ate it languidly, breaking its puffed crust with her spoon so it sagged, lathering it with whipped cream, letting the flavor of each long mouthful absorb her fully, exclusively.

They drove back to Rockaway. Marty pulled up to Nana's house; Sarah opened the door, stepped out, and waved good-bye while he was in mid-argument with Tony over a proposed shift in their harmony. He nodded briefly at her, said Yeah, bye, glad you came, call you tomorrow, but the next day he didn't.

The days went by.

She called her parents, to check in, as she'd been meaning to; her father had just returned from his twelfth in a series of thirty radiation treatments, and described for her, again, in detail, getting his groin tattooed for it, how they'd marked him with indigo dots to help line up the machine for the lasers. There's just a little burn during the actual treatment, he told her; the only thing to really hurt, so far, was getting the tattoo. Mainly he's tired from it, wiped out, not all there, only played nine holes this morning, No, your mom's fine, I guess, looks like she'll get back on the transplant list, we'll see . . . how's your painting coming, honey, we miss you, where do you get those little square batteries for the smoke detectors, your mother can't find them, we're hoping there's no fire while you're gone, when are you coming home? He began to describe for her how the medication turns his urine a bright cherry red, but she cut in to say she had to go, she'll call them again soon, really. Her mother got on the phone to say Your father's no help at all, I'm sick, too, I'm yellow, you should see, what is he blaming me for, my head is throbbing, we miss you, honey, I got an overdraft notice from the bank but it makes no sense, I need you to go through the statement with me, we love you, how's your painting coming, when are you coming home? She said she'd call again in a few days, Really, yes, I promise, I love you, too, and hung up.

Twice a day she forces herself out of Nana's house, deliberately leaves her phone behind, feels satisfaction that Bernadette, having left for Sri Lanka, isn't around to answer any calls on the house phone. She bicycles to the store for a single apple or a carton of yogurt, or maneuvers her way down the invaded, noisy beach, bits of lemon pulp drying in her hair. She steps carefully around the broken shells, the litter, the washed-up jellyfish that look like clear embryonic sacs of fluid with feathery red stars in the center, sets as her goal the towering lifeguard chair roughly twelve blocks' distance down from Nana's, looking for the raised red flag and the promise of danger, and directly in front of what she has figured is Marty's living room window overlooking the shore. She inquires the time of the lifeguard, a golden, cool-authority college kid flipping his whistle lanyard like a lariat, so obviously happy with this awesome summer gig of his, questions him about the starry jellyfish—do they sting? Are there riptides, here, bad undertows?—and stands there peering up at him, resolutely facing the water. She dips a toe in, lets the cool surf swirl past her feet, but the ocean itself is strangely uninviting. She can't imagine just plunging in to all that cold dark deep.

She trudges back home to do slow stretching and abdominal toning exercises on the sandy floor of her room. Her untouched canvases slant in stacks against the walls; her easel, holding her still-only-begun painting of the little shell, stands to one side like a sentinel. She thinks it isn't a strong beginning, after all. She thinks about painting it out, starting again. She thinks about switching it for a fresh clean canvas, starting all over. She decides it would be a waste to give up on it, though, now that it's already actually begun. She reminds herself it is still only July. There is still plenty of time. She turns all of her canvases to face the wall, to avoid their reproachful stares.

Her phone doesn't ring until five-thirty the following Friday afternoon, when Marty calls her to tell her what time he'll pick her up for shabbes dinner at Itzak's. Fuck you, she thinks as he talks, Fuck you and your loud musician friends and your fanatical religious friends and your insulting self-absorption. What am I doing? she thinks, gazing at her canvas, this is such bullshit, dioxazine purple, that's what it needs, I'll just stay home tonight and paint. That's what you're supposed to be doing, yes. She tells him she can't possibly be ready by seven-thirty, she'll just meet him there at eight. She rides her bike to the store—the third time that day—to buy a bottle of Baron Herzog Chardonnay, and breezes into Itzak and Darlene's with it at eight-fifteen, after the candles are already lit and just as Marty and Itzak are launching into a vigorous rendition of *Shalom Aleichem*, the whole family pounding the table like enraptured idiots. Itzak says Kiddush over the wine, and everyone troops to the kitchen to wash their hands. She ignores Marty during dinner, instead plying Itzak and Darlene's son Jonah with questions about junior high, and their skinny daughter Gwen with questions about her classes at NYU and what she hopes are borderline-inappropriate questions about cute boys. She drinks glass after glass of Baron Herzog, pours it for herself when Itzak lags in his hostly duty, and wonders if Gwen, despite the miniskirts and pierced ears, has ever had sex, ever seen a real penis, ever even kissed a guy. She eyes Darlene's bobbed hair and wonders if it really is just a clever wig. She wonders if Jonah masturbates. She wonders what Itzak's beard must taste like, if Itzak and Darlene have sex through a hole in a sheet, if he fucks her with his yarmulke on, if he shuns her during her period then makes her go to the mikvah to ritually bathe away all the filth. She suddenly hates Jews.

———

"YOU OUGHTTA COME to my place for shabbes lunch tomorrow," he says as he walks her home.

"What?" she says, nonplussed.

"I'll make you lunch. I get home from shul by eleven, so you come over around noon, right?"

"I have too much work to do," she says. "I don't have time."

"But it's Saturday. I'll make us lunch."

"I'm in the middle of a painting, I don't want to lose the momentum."

"Oh, come on. Just lunch, right?"

They stop outside Nana's house; she steps up on the curb, so they're eye to eye. He looks hopeful, and it quickens her, kills her resolve.

"Yeah, okay." They regard each other a moment; she quickly leans over and kisses him on the cheek. His arms enfold her unexpectedly, clasping her. She feels clasped. It's both feeling trapped and feeling held, safe, and confuses her for a moment; she tries to pull away.

"Wait," he says. She waits, and he takes a deep breath, releasing it into her hair. "Why aren't you breathing?" he asks. So she takes a deep showy breath, releases it, and her body involuntarily sags against him, her face in the collar of his jacket, the sweetish leather brine. "Yeah, that's it," he says. Then releases her so unexpectedly she almost stumbles off the curb. "So, you'll be there? I can't call you tomorrow to check."

"Okay, yes, I'll be there."

"Good," he says, and ambles off.

⌒

THERE ARE PHOTOS everywhere: Marty with his son at age six, at ten, at fourteen, at eighteen, Marty with his old bands, Marty onstage, Marty with Tony and Frankie and Sammy, Marty with Julius. Crammed among the photos are books: *Jewish History and Spirituality*, the Torah, Talmud, *Biblical Literacy*, *Jewish Ritual*, *The Living Jew*, *The Jew in America*, *Zen Judaism*, *Modern Judaism*, *The Jewish Mystical Tradition*, *Jews in Hollywood*, *Jews in Music*, *Jews in Rock and Roll*, and a section devoted to the Holocaust, Primo Levi, Elie Wiesel, Hannah Arendt, Franz Rosenzweig, Martin Buber,

Hasidism, the history of Israel. Then shelf after shelf of record albums, thousands of them, labeled and chronologized, subdivided alphabetically, smelling of old cardboard turning slowly to dust. The dining room table is set with straw place mats and nice china, tiny crystal glasses with silver filigree, a challah ready for slicing. The two lighted white candles flicker as she passes.

"This is really nice," Sarah tells him.

He beams at her as he carries in a bowl of salad. "Yeah? It's good, right? Twenty-five years, I been here." The dining room window looks out on the beach, a gleam of white sand and blue water, the throng of beachgoers, the lifeguard in his high chair down near the water's break framed perfectly, asymmetrically, exactly as she'd pictured.

"Did you live here with your wife and son?"

He blinks at the light, turns back to her. "No, I bought it after me and Barbara split up. Daniel, he went back and forth, you know? Barbara lives in Ohio. She's a realtor."

"Where's your son now?"

"My son. My son is off doing his thing. Daniel's living in Tel Aviv with his wife, a real sabra. You think *I'm* a fanatic. Man. He's a record producer, all the digital stuff. He's off doing, living his life. Here, I made a salad. And there's hard boiled eggs, you like those?"

"It's fine. It's great. I know, no cooking. I didn't expect a pork roast." He rolls his eyes at her, and she realizes, pleased, that he's nervous. She'd dressed deliberately: thin-strapped tank top and her shortest shorts, a pair of boy's flannel boxers. Her bare legs gleam smooth with baby oil; the skin of her naked arms, she notes with satisfaction, looks golden, unmarred. He's wearing shorts and a baggy T-shirt, high-top sneakers, just as she's seen him dressed for playing handball. A backward baseball cap on his head, the name of some movie embroidered above the bill. "Is that what you wear to shul?" she asks.

"No, I changed when I got back. Oh, wait, here . . . " He opens a misty, iced bottle of vodka, half-fills her little crystal glass, tops it off with a dash from a bottle of pinkish liquid. "Apricot schnapps. Daniel brings it from Israel when he comes." He recites a quick Kiddush in Hebrew while she watches, then hands her the glass. "You'll like this, here."

She drinks it down, feels it crawl through her chest like a hot crab. "Mm. That's nice."

"Good. Here, you'll have more . . . " He pours her another one, swallows his. He glances at her shoulders, her legs, and she resists the reflexive urge to turn away, to cross her arms or step behind a chair to cover her thighs. She sips from her glass, steps slowly out of her sandals, and scratches the back of one calf with a toe. "You okay in those?" he asks, nodding at her sandals on the floor. "After lunch we'll go for a walk."

"Are we allowed to do that?"

"Yeah, sure. It counts as *menuchah*. Rest. Itzak says it's a mitzvah, taking a stroll on shabbes. A mitzvah's—"

"I know, a blessing."

"No, see, that's what people *think* mitzvoh means. But a mitzvah's more like a commandment. A sacred deed. The mitzvoh, see, those're what we *do*, the actions we perform that bring holiness, spirituality."

"And shabbes is the day to load up on them."

"Yeah, that's right. Good. Like going to shul. Lighting the candles. Like taking a long stroll with someone so you can just, you know, *be* together." He fills her tiny glass again with vodka, another dash of schnapps, and smiles at her with pleasure. "Like inviting someone into your home."

———

THEY STROLL A mile or so down the beach, through Riis Park, past the mobbed handball courts and bicycle paths, around the teeming families picnicking, barbecuing on every grassy inch of space. Even the air is too crowded, here, full of roasting meat, onion, mustard smells, the blare and throb of boom boxes, people laughing, chattering.

"And with the transplant, she'll be good again, your mom?" he asks.

"I guess. Although if I were a person with Hepatitis C or

something I'd be pretty pissed off if they wasted a perfectly good liver giving it to a sixty-two-year-old alcoholic."

He waves a hand at her, dismisses her comment as a joke. "But your dad's there, see, that's good. They got each other."

"Yeah, but they keep trying to outsick each other. Whoever's more miserable wins. And he plays a lot of golf. He leaves to go play golf a lot." She stops to adjust her sandal.

"What do you want to do?" Marty asks. "You getting tired? You want to keep going, or turn around? Head home?"

"No, let's just stop for a moment." They head up onto the boardwalk, the warped wooden slats creaking beneath their feet. They pause at a bench, and sit, facing the ocean, pigeons fluttering away.

"Yeah, but still," he continues, "that's the thing about growing old together, you know? You take care of your kids, then you take care of each other, and then the kids, right, there's a point it turns around and your kids start helping you. That's really the beautiful thing, taking care of your parents. Like you do. Honoring them. Doing back for them everything they did for you. It's a mitzvah."

"Yes," she says. She feels a twinge of resentment, for his ludicrous little mythology. "But little kids need help, they need all that attention and support, for what, ten years, fifteen years? And the whole time parents are raising the kids *toward* growing up. Toward independence. For everybody. That's the direction it goes, right, the goal? So parents get more and more free. The other way around, when the parents get older, you just get more and more trapped there. Trapped on that path. And who knows for how long?"

"Huh," he says. "But you said they were doing okay. With you gone. They're doing fine, right?"

"Yeah, for now. Like, today. But each day, as they get older and worse, it's just . . . looming. How horrible it's going to get. They're going to need more and more help, and I'll be more and more . . . " She pauses. She must sound terrible to him, she realizes, so insensitive and indifferent to her parents' suffering. "I mean, I'm just trying to appreciate the time we have left together. And it's worse for them. I'm worried for *them*. I just don't want them to be miserable. I don't want them to suffer."

"Yeah, sure. I get what you mean. It's scary."

They look out at the ocean. A ship is passing in the distance, and she remembers the moment of her early days here, the bright view from her window. Seagulls swoop in arcs, set in perfect composition against the clouds. The water is darkening in the late-afternoon sun, the waves beginning to shadow and peak in the tide.

"So, who takes care of you?" he asks out of nowhere.

"What?" she says. "I'm fine. I'm not the one who needs caretaking, thank God." He can be so oblivious, she thinks, for all his soul-filled books and questions and spiritual crusades. She looks away from him, grips the bench, feels her throat grow tight. This happened before, she thinks, clenching her jaw, that first night at Itzak's with him, talking about, what, shells, pearls, the soul, something about pudding. And then when she fell on the bike outside his house, what she thought was his house, but it wasn't, he wasn't there, and she cried there in the street like some pathetic little girl. Why be with someone who makes you want to cry because he's there, who makes you want to cry because he isn't there? Why even bother?

She unexpectedly feels his hand on the back of her neck; he slides his fingers up, spreads them across the back of her skull, lifting her hair from its damp roots. The sudden breeze there makes her feel crept into, seen through. She feels transparent as gloss gel, and she wants to keep on resenting him, wants its opaque brace.

"But I am going to leave soon," she says. "I'm leaving," she says.

"You are?" He looks disturbed.

"My friend Emily's having a baby in a few weeks, and I get to be there. I'm the doula."

"What's that?"

"Well, the midwife's busy doing all the baby and birth stuff, so the doula's there to, I don't know, give the mother backrubs. Get the ice cream and anchovies. Tend to her."

"Wow," he says slowly.

"She's having a water birth. In a big tub in the living room."

He looks at her as if she's making this up. "But, how's that work? The baby in the water like that?"

"It's only for a few seconds. The baby's still getting oxygen from the mom, through the cord. They're still connected like that. Emily says it's less traumatic for the baby, actually. Like a mellower, more natural transition to entering the cold cruel world and figuring out how to breathe all on its own."

"Wow," he says again. "Okay. But after all that, you'll come back?"

"I don't know." She shrugs. His eyebrows are lifted in hope and distress, and she likes it.

"No, come on, you'll come back, right?"

"Maybe I'll come back." She tips her head back into his cradling hand. "For a while."

———

MARTY SHOWS HER the upstairs of his house: guest room, office, master bedroom, all window'd and full of the same seashell hum as her room at Nana's. His bathtub is a thick, deep square of creamy veined marble with an ocean view, gold-chromed, fluted spigot and Jacuzzi jets, surrounded by glass bowls full of sea sponges and bath soaps shaped like colorful scallops.

"Very Hugh Hefner," she tells him.

He leans against the doorjamb, sheepish. "Yeah," he says. "I just put this in a few years ago. Wish I'd had it before. When I was young enough to really enjoy it."

"Aw," she says. Her tank top is sticking to her back; she suddenly feels dirty, aware of all the sweat. She thinks she smells like old egg. "Hey, can I take a bath?'

"What?"

"Can I take a bath in that thing? Let me take a bath."

"Yeah, sure." He straightens up, interested in this abrupt project. "Those towels are clean," he says, motioning to a neat, folded pile, "and here, you push this for the jets . . . " He turns the faucets on full blast, and points out a button to push.

"Do you have any bubble bath?"

"Uh, yeah. I do." He selects a bottle from a large wire basket, offers it to her to sniff.

Cucumber, clover maybe, sweet lemon. "That's good."

He squeezes in a pint; she pushes on the jets, and the water turns to scented froth. "So, uh . . . yeah," he says, waving fingers at her. "Have fun." He leaves, sliding the bathroom door closed behind him.

She strips off her tank top and shorts, her underwear. She steps in the tub, the hot foam already rising to her knees. She sits, opening her legs, scooping water under her arms.

"You need anything?" she hears him yell.

"Yeah," she yells back, over the jets. "Bring me something to drink."

She settles back as the warm water floats up her arms, her shoulders, bubbling up to her throat. She turns off the faucet, then the jets. Her body floats like the jellyfish in the tide pools. I live on the beach, she thinks, it's right there, the whole entire beautiful ocean, and I never even go in. I should, this is so lovely, floating. Her hair drifts off, darkening in the water, and she thinks of seaweed; she slides her hands up across her scalp, pulling the hair out further, letting it soak, getting so dark now, used to be so blond when she was little, at least all the sun and lemons are helping.

She floats.

She wishes there were a big tub like this at Nana's, so she could float this way every day, be cleanly buoyant. She lets her head drop back until the water covers her ears, so she can have all the peace of being inside water. She recalls some portrait in some gallery—Germany? England? Late sixteenth-century, a Holbein knock-off in an unbefitting Baroque gold frame—of some blood-bathing Countess who killed hundreds of virgins so she could soak in a vast bath of their blood, convinced of its rejuvenating potential, its power to keep her young. The portrait showed a beautiful but viper-faced woman around thirty, with milky, unstained skin and aureate blond hair, an angelic smile. She wonders how long the Countess lived, if she ever ran out of virgins, if she died retaining her youthful, venous blush.

There's a knock, she hears that, faintly, and the door slides open again; Marty hands her a tiny, silver-filigreed crystal glass of cold pinkish liquid, a copy of *Newsday*, a rolled towel for her neck. He places a clean, folded T-shirt on the sink.

"This is so nice," Sarah says. "This is perfect." She sits up to take everything from him, the water dipping to nipple level, her throat and chest covered in bubbled, sliding foam. "I am never leaving. I am staying here for the rest of my life."

"Don't," he says, leaving again, waving his hand at her. "Don't do that to me."

WHEN SHE PADS damply back to his room an hour later, wearing his T-shirt and her flannel boxer shorts, he's on his bed, asleep. Curled on his side like a tuckered-out little boy, amid a pile of pillows and magazines. He's changed his baseball cap to a black knit one, with a tiny pompom on top. She tosses her underwear and tank top at the foot of the bed and climbs up, gently, on the side of his backbone's convex curve. She finds an old *Rolling Stone*, props herself against the headboard, reads. She wishes she'd gone downstairs, first, for another vodka-and-schnapps, but she likes the composition, doesn't want to move again. The wall of his room facing the ocean is floor-to-ceiling glass, leading out to a small balcony; there's a beautiful, dimming light coming through, the shadows just beginning to angle. She hears seagulls, and the muted sounds of families leaving the beach, a soothing, tranquil noise.

Marty stirs, rolls to his other side, facing her. "Hey," he says when he notices her, as if surprised.

"Hey," she says.

"How was your bath?"

"Lovely." She smiles briefly at him, goes back to the article on Elvis Costello.

"What time is it?" His little cap is askew, he adjusts it, then rubs his eyes.

"Around five, I think."

"I should go to shul."

"Okay. I'll get going." She puts the magazine down and turns to crawl off the bed, but he grasps her wrist.

"No, wait."

"Why?"

"Come here." He tugs her back down, positions her so she's on her side, facing away from him. He crimps his knees behind hers, wraps an arm around her shoulders, holds her close. She counts to ten in her head, very slowly, like giving a child plenty of time to hide, then tenses as if to leave. His arm instantly tightens, his hand at her throat, and she smiles to herself. "Don't go, yet," he mumbles.

"Okay."

His hand travels slowly down the front of her shirt, across her waist, to her hip, and stops at the edge of flannel and skin. She feels fingers brush the hem of her shorts. Then stop.

"This isn't exactly uncle and niece," she says after a moment.

"What?"

"That's how you usually treat me. Like an uncle and niece."

"Wow," he says. "I do?" His hand slips just inside her shorts, palms itself flat against her buttock.

"Well," she says, shifting her legs.

"Okay, stop talking now," he says.

She smiles, waiting. She feels her heart thumping against his arm, and hopes he doesn't notice. She waits for the crept-into feeling of his hand at the back of her neck, his fingers in her hair, steadying her. She tries to slow her breathing to match and keep pace with his, until she realizes, from the deepening, slowing feel of his chest rising and falling against her shoulder, that he has once again fallen back to sleep.

THE CONNECTICUT COUNTRYSIDE in autumn is Sarah's favorite—the smell of stripped corn, the orange, yellow, and green plaid of trees. Moons that hang low and burn through a haze of chaff and dust. The ducklings have grown glossy over the summer, and waddle around the grounds; the sheep's wool has grown in enough from spring shearing to gather burrs and a confetti of hay. They bleat inscrutably when she passes by to collect eggs, or rip beans from their twining vines in the arbor. It isn't really autumn yet—still early August, she knows there's time left—but it's beyond the flush of summer; the oversized fruits and vegetables in Emily's garden have peaked, and Sarah feels a hurry to use everything so the lushness isn't left to rot. Rubbery zucchini, wilting lettuces, old, uncracked eggs, leathered melons—every day she dumps more used and unused food on the compost heap, which rises to slow, decaying prominence in a far corner of the yard.

Emily is nine days overdue, and the household is on chaotic edge, waiting.

The doula, Sarah reads in the dog-eared pregnancy and childbirth books sagging a kitchen shelf, is the primary female caretaker of the mother-to-be during late pregnancy, labor, and delivery; the midwife arrives only when contractions are reliably prompt and severe, expecting advanced cervical dilation and lots of snacks, and the coach—Emily's solemn husband, Michael—is himself fully involved in the birth experience. But the doula, while often a dear friend, is still an outsider, a woman who can focus solely on the birthing mother's needs and wants. This, Sarah is happy to interpret, means the fun stuff.

The housework is done by a nervous young woman in her twenties, who comes twice a week and talks compulsively to Sarah about her coming and going boyfriends; Rachel and Elijah are cared for by their nanny, a mammoth, fleshy grandmother of seven with a blond crew cut, who eight hours a day joshes them out of their whines, listens to Rachel chant her loop of "Baa Baa Black Sheep," walks them around out of doors searching for dragonfly wings, and lets them ride her like a horse. Being a doula means keeping to the fringe of that, not disrupting the settled flow of the house with her presence—her job is the garnish, to provide distraction and simple comforts. She rubs Emily's feet with peppermint lotion, brushes out and braids her hair, stirs curry powder and gobs of soy mayonnaise into her favorite scrambled eggs. She takes the bags full of the wool shorn from the three sheep—Messy Marv, Sophia, and Brian—to the carding lady, who teaches her about vegetable-based dyes and shows her how to spin fibers to yarn on a wooden, foot-pedaled wheel. She takes the bored family dog for long, deep-lung'd walks in the woods surrounding Emily's house, and checks him for ticks. She joins Michael when he is tense and exhausted for cocktail-hour glasses of McCallan 18 whiskey, pops in a reggae CD, and asks him about his day while Emily naps. She fills a wheelbarrow of basil from the garden and makes pesto, scooping cups of it into recycled yogurt containers for freezing. She picks too-ripe blackberries until the juice stains her cuticles like blood, as if she'd tried to claw her way out of a pit.

She picks up the creamy, fluffy curls of wool from the carding lady, and Emily, whose fingers are swollen, hands over knitting needles so Sarah can get to work on this year's sweaters for the family. She stretches out on the living room sofa with Emily, knitting, humming, massaging the dog's stiff-haired belly with her toes.

"Was he ever married, this guy? Does he have any kids?" Emily asks, drinking juice.

"One son. I think he's twenty-eight or nine." Marty has shown her a recent photo: his son, a stunning version of a much-younger Marty, dancing unabashedly at some wild tribal event.

"He must've gotten married pretty young."

"Yep." Sarah smiles over her needles at Emily. "He got married the year before you and I were born."

"Well, you know, it's what they did back then. Marry young," says Emily, poking Sarah in the thigh with her foot. "You know, in that generation."

"He's still friends with his ex-wife."

"That's good. That's a sign of maturity."

"Oh, just what I need. Another sign of his maturity."

"Is that the wool from Messy Marv?"

"Uh huh." Sarah holds up her work; rows of knitted wool are lining up like a furrowed field. "The pullover for Rachel."

"Pretty."

She puts her knitting down, and takes the juice glass from Emily. "Should we do your stomach again?"

"Yeah, sure. Thanks. Is that stuff still okay, you think? It's leftover from Elijah."

Sarah sniffs at a bottle of apricot oil. "It's fine. Maybe a little funky. It's fine." She slides a pillow under Emily's knees, helps pull off her splotched blouse. She pours oil into her palm, warms it a moment, smoothes it in expanding, then decreasing concentric circles on Emily's swollen basket of an abdomen.

Emily takes a deep breath, and gazes up at the ceiling. "Two more days, and the midwife won't let me deliver at home," she says. "Maybe I should swim more laps. Get on the Stairmaster."

"Or a trampoline. A pogo stick."

"You can do that harder."

"I don't want to hurt you."

"That's okay. This isn't supposed to feel wonderful." Emily sighs. "It's meant to be persuasive."

Sarah pushes her palm with more force, feeling what must be baby foot, baby arm, baby skull. "Are you still going with 'Ariel'?"

"Yep. 'Lion of God.' That is, of course, assuming he or she is ever actually born." Emily balls her fists, and shoves them under the small of her back. Her naked breasts slip sideways.

"Here . . . " Sarah adjusts the pillow under Emily's knees. "I'd be so freaked out. But maybe it's easier, each time? Does it get easier?"

"I think it gets *worse*. I know what's coming. I know this really horrendous thing is going to happen, rip up my body and be really traumatic, and there's nothing I can do about it. It's absolutely inevitable."

"Sounds like being on death row. Waiting for the firing squad."

"Sort of, yeah. Woop . . . " A droplet of milk spills from her right breast to the couch. "That hasn't happened in a while. Can you hand me a diaper?"

"Yeah, here. Wait, this one's a little vomity."

"That's okay."

"The other one, too." Sarah motions to Emily's left nipple, where milk is beading up. She watches Emily tuck the diaper under her breasts; they look full and stretched out, and Sarah thinks of wind socks, of how they start to sag just at the moment the breeze first dies, somehow sagging while still taut and weighted with air. In high school, in college, Emily's body was a picture, the loveliest, unblemished thing. She remembers coveting that body. The body, and Emily's attitude toward it, blithe, unaware. She used to draw Emily naked, in tribute. A 2B Conte soft crayon for shading the longish lines and curves, a 1 or 2H to get the fine points, an eyelash, a fingernail, a nipple's crinkled nub. The light from their dorm room window glowing over Emily's plummy, lissome nakedness; Sarah, skinny and shapeless, drawing her, both of them drinking jug Chablis and analyzing Fauvist art, agonizing over boys, being silly and so-serious and young. A book they'd do together some day, a feminist reinterpretation of fairy tales, Emily writing the text, a series of prose poems, Sarah drawing mock and ironic Pre-Raphaelite heroines in pen and ink. But it would be so different to draw her now. Capture that drummed-flat navel and slumped breasts, the distorted spine, the pearly streaks of stretch marks. The recline on a couch out of weariness and strain. Sarah straightens her own spine and looks down at her own legs, glowing with vibrancy and health, in good shape from all the bicycling and long strolls around Rockaway. She helps Emily mop up milk.

"Thanks. So, tell me stories. I picture this guy quoting Kabbalah at you all the time."

"No," Sarah says, smiling. "He doesn't do that." She pours more apricot oil, returns to orbiting Emily's belly with a greased hand. "But he gets up every morning at six-thirty to daven."

"Sarah."

"I know."

"I cannot picture this," says Emily. "You and this guy."

"There's nothing to picture. He just likes having me hover around. I'm just entourage."

"So why don't you start something? If you want it to happen."

"But I *don't*. I don't think I do . . . " She is confused, made uneasy by his lack of initiative, by the blurriness between them. She has thought of starting it, yes, but she senses if she is too assertive, too sexual, he'll just be appalled, see baseness, cast her away with some righteous biblical injunction. "This guy's too weird. It's too complicated. It isn't about sex," she says. And it *isn't*, she thinks. It's something else, there is something else they must be getting at, but she doesn't know what. It is unrecognizable, it feels like maybe a place to rest, it is a joke she can make, it is fraught.

"It's not like it was with David," she says, finally.

"But that's all it was with David."

"Yeah. It was so simple. So well-defined. Clean margins. I miss that."

"Well, maybe when you go home again . . . "

She brushes the idea away with an oily hand. "I'm too old for David. He was just a kid. All starting out and eager and excited about everything. He was like a little boy."

"And so now you're dating Methuselah."

"Ha." She mock-raps her knuckles on Emily's belly. "Ha ha."

"Just see what happens with this one. Sounds like he adores you."

"No, I don't think he does. Maybe part of the time."

"Maybe he's frightened."

"I think he's just wildly conflicted. I think he's a mess. Hey, it's summer, it's the beach, it's something to do. Just fun, like you said."

Emily nods. She puts her hand over Sarah's, and they rub her belly together a moment. She gazes out the living room window toward the garden. "We should probably bring in the rest of the Swiss chard soon, if it's still good. It's been so hot, everything's just about compost by now."

"I'll go out later," Sarah says. "We should finish what's left of the raspberries, too. Before the birds do." She gets up and tugs open a window, draws the muslin curtains apart to catch any of the late afternoon breeze. They listen to the rasping pulse of insect wings.

"Emily?" Michael enters, looking dazed and rumpled, carrying Elijah pouched in front of him like an infant marsupial. "Honey, are you having the new baby now?"

"No."

"Then, can you take him? He's hungry. And I really need a nap. Can this be my time for a nap?"

"Yeah, hand him over," Emily says wearily. Michael

pulls the baby free from the pouch's straps, and Sarah passes him to Emily.

"Come here, baby boy," says Emily. "Baby, baby boy . . . hey, where's Rachel?" she calls.

"Aggie took her to feed the ducklings," he calls back, as he stumbles from the room.

Emily settles Elijah around her bulk, and molds her nearest breast toward him. She brushes his lips with a brown, pulled-long nipple; he clamps on happily.

She watches Emily nurse. She likes watching this, the world goes sleepy and peaceful. This, is pretty. This would be nice to draw, she thinks, those soft, intimate lines. Maybe there're some colored pencils around somewhere. Rachel must have a drawerful of paints and brushes, maybe do it as a watercolor.

"Should I stop with the oil?" she asks.

"No, we should go the whole twenty minutes."

"Okay." Sarah resumes looping her hand around hard, around, around. The light's good for another hour, she thinks. I could even get some fresh eggs from the henhouse, mix up some kind of organic tempera paint. Saturated colors. Very Giotto, very Madonna-and-Child . . .

"Just promise me if anything *does* get started, you'll be careful. Don't let this happen to you." Emily looks down at the tracks of oil on her belly, shiny as rain-slicked pavement, and Sarah smiles.

"Don't worry. That, I am religious about. And I'm still on the pill, anyway, so . . . " Emily looks mildly disapproving. "I know, I know. Don't say it." She thinks about moving Emily closer to the window for a better composition. Taking her long hair out of that ratty braid, letting it float and curl over her shoulders in golden light. So pretty. Like a della Francesca.

"You know, my homeopath has all these natural hormonal birth control things. If you want to talk to her. And I could show you how to check your mucus, know when you're fertile, know when it's safe."

"No, thanks. I'm not taking any chances."

"I just hate you being on that stuff all these years. What it could be doing to your body."

It's better than these stretch marks of yours, Sarah thinks, but doesn't say. Better than ripping up your body, yes. "I'm not worried," she says.

"And how it might affect your system, down the road. If you ever change your mind about kids."

"Now that, I'm *really* not worried about," she says.

"Yeah." Emily smiles. "You sort of already have two kids."

"Exactly."

"It's funny. I was thinking about that, after we talked the other day. How there's this weird paradox in your life."

"What do you mean?"

"Well, there's your parents, and what happened after

Aaron. You had to grow up so fast, to take care of them. And that made you so—"

"I know, I know. You think I shouldn't feel so responsible for them."

"No, responsible *about* them."

"All right, whatever. I agree. It's highly dysfunctional." She gives an elaborately resigned shrug. "But it's not forever."

"No, that's not it. I was thinking how it also keeps you, it's *kept* you, your whole life, in this place where you get to stay the child. At the same time."

Her oil-rubbing hand on Emily's belly stops. "What do you mean?"

"Well, parents are a kid's whole emotional focus, right? That's what home is. Parents create this emotional space the child can live and feel secure in. An extension of the womb. And venturing out of that is frightening. To separate, and be out in the world. Having to create all that space for yourself. Forge your own path. You've never had to do that. I'm being figurative, but—"

"But Em, that's not true! Come on . . ." She hears her voice waver, and tries to lighten her tone, go lilting and carefree. "I am *here*, look? Right? I have ventured from my literal *and* figurative home. I *have* forged. I'm not a child."

"I know, that's what I was getting to. You took this huge leap, and now you're, well, unstuck. I guess I've always been more worried how you'd deal with stuff *after* they're gone. When that focus is taken away, all that investment, like, *then* what's Sarah going to do? On her own, with all her own life to live on her own terms. And now you're doing it. I'm really proud of you."

You know what real sin is? she remembers. *Inertia. Refusing the responsibility for your own life.*

She looks away from Emily's encouraging smile. It feels so condescending, her praise. Her pity. "I don't get why you had to be so worried, Em. Of course I'm doing it. It just had to be the right time." She rubs, firmly, circling, circling. "I told you about my shell painting, right?"

"Yeah. It sounds beautiful."

"The *paintings*, I mean. I've started a whole series, actually." She clears her throat, pictures her single canvas, her lonely little shell. The untouched blots of drying paint on her palette. Her faceless, empty canvases turned away and leaning against the walls of her room. "It's all about shells and hidden undersea lives. What can live without air, then dies when it comes to the surface. Challenging our assumptions about what sustains and nourishes us. That kind of paradox." She waves her hands in the air, in what she hopes demonstrates paradox and insight. "Very elemental."

"I can't wait to see them."

"It's amazing, how everything's really coming along

now. Being away from home, being here, it's all been so . . . generative. Really defining. So don't worry about me, all right? I'm fine. I'm doing it. I'm in the groove."

Emily nods, thinking. "The truth is . . . " she pauses, "you were always the talented one. You were blessed that way. I used to be so jealous."

"Oh," Sarah says. She looks away from Emily's gaze, pushes her hands back onto her belly. "Well, thanks."

"So, when's the exhibit happening? Is there a date set? Michael and I can escape the kids for a few days maybe, come out for it? I'd love to be there."

"It's not really that definite, yet. I'll want to show her all the work I've done here, the whole series, first. The woman with the gallery. Consult with her about the details, the framing, the installation. It's still way down the road. Don't worry, I'll let you guys know."

A faint eggy smell breezes in. Probably the compost, she thinks. She removes her hand from Emily's belly to stretch her arms for a moment, flex her own bones. Emily drinks some juice, then offers up the glass.

"You want some more?" Sarah asks.

"No, for you. Go ahead and finish it."

Sarah swallows the last of the juice. "Hey," she tells Emily, "you know, maybe you could write the text for the catalog? Would you like that?"

"Sure, I'd love to."

She smiles, puts her hand back on Emily's stomach, slides slow hard circles, hard, harder.

"You can stop if you want," Emily says. "Really."

"No, I like doing this."

"I did also think, though . . . " Emily drifts her hand across Elijah's forehead. "After Rachel was born, and then now, I do think there's one part about having kids that you'd really like—"

"Look, I know I'm missing out. It's the most primally important life experience there is, right? I get that. But I've got so much other stuff going on in my life, I just—"

"Believe me, Sarah, I'm not proselytizing. But *this* part, I mean. This is my favorite. This is the best." Emily kisses the top of Elijah's head.

"Breastfeeding?"

"It isn't like a guy doing it. It's totally different."

"It must be an amazing feeling."

"You want to?"

Sarah's hand stops in mid-circuit. "Breastfeed Elijah?"

"Sure. See what it feels like."

"I don't exactly have any milk."

"Neither do I. He's sucking down colostrum, now. Anyway, I told you, it's more of a comfort thing for him. The closeness."

"I don't know . . . " The idea of baring her own small breast, of tucking her tiny pink point of a nipple into his baby mouth, feels all wrong. Fraudulent. Like a little girl playacting, outside-the-lines lipstick stolen from a big sister's drawer, high-heeled shoes sneaked from a mommy's closet, spooning pretend food into a baby doll's hard plastic mouth. She feels faintly queasy, must be that smell, compost and baby vomit, this rancid oil.

There's a sudden, lumpy throb beneath her hand, knobbing Emily's belly. "Hey," Sarah says, laughing, "take it easy, kid. We know you're in there."

"Any time, Ariel," Emily says tiredly. "We're ready and waiting. We're excited to meet you. Any time you're ready." She pulls her nipple from Elijah's baby-drunk face, and dabs at his chin with the diaper. "It does make me a little sad, I guess," she says to Sarah. "That you'll miss out on this."

Actually, it's a cliché, isn't it? Sarah thinks, studying her. "Nursing Mother," too banal, like a subway ad for La Leche League. A cheesy Hallmark Mother's Day card. All those relentless Mary-and-baby-Jesus icons. No, she can't paint Emily now. She is supposed to find her beautiful this way, she knows, still beautiful, even more beautiful, a woman's body ripe with fruit, performing this miraculous function, pregnancy, birth, but what has happened to this body is just awful. So sad. She can't draw her in tribute now, it would be something else. It wouldn't be kind. Like an anatomical study, faintly Darwinian. She's aesthetically distasteful, now. Scarred. That ugly brown line bisecting her abdomen, down to the pubic bone, a leftover from her two previous pregnancies; it looks like a trail of ants, Sarah thinks, crushed by a careless foot.

"Sarah?" Emily strains to raise up Elijah's slack, sleepy body, to hand him over, offering him. "You want to? Yes?"

"No. Thanks, but . . . " *The most important thing in the world*, she can hear herself recite generously to Emily, but it isn't. It's the most *common* thing in the world, farcically pedestrian. It's no great achievement, anybody can have a baby, be a mother, idiots, drunks, teenagers, dogs, there's no singular or sacred experience here.

"You sure?" Emily's kind smile is maddening, a complacent smirk.

She's trying so hard to offer me something, Sarah thinks, but I'm the one who has it all. I'm just here visiting this life, but she's stuck in it, she's trapped. I get to leave when I want. I'm the one with all the freedom, all the choices, the blessings, like she says, the incredible paintings to do, the real achievement, future, an exciting, unencumbered life all my own ahead of me.

"I don't think so," Sarah says. "But thanks."

"You really can, if you want to."

That drifting, putrid odor again, cloying. "You smell that?" she asks Emily. "That's awful. I think the compost is too close to the house. It's encroaching. It's taking over the garden." Sarah laughs shortly, gets up, and pulls the curtains fully closed against the smell. "I'm going to go bring in the chard. Should we have it for dinner? Do that thing with the garlic?"

There's always such a difference, she thinks, leaving without waiting for Emily to answer, between not having a choice—and having a choice but choosing no.

———

WHEN THE CONTRACTIONS first start, just after eight that night, Sarah goes to the darkening garden and selects a grotesquely oversized and rubbery zucchini, which takes her forty minutes to grate. In between spooning batches of green-flecked batter into loaf pans, she refills glasses of juice for Emily, presses down hard with an orange on her sacrum, and, with Michael, helps her pace the living room near the birthing tub. She pours herself a large glass of McCallan 18 over ice and sips it while she makes nine loaves of zucchini bread, factoring in one for the midwife to snack on during labor, and two to take home with her afterward in thanks, like a party favor. Aggie brings Rachel and Elijah into the kitchen, and slices them thick sweet hunks from the family loaves, spread with butter. Sometime after midnight Nana, balancing on her walker like a pro, and Emily's parents Leah and Sid, her aunt Rose and cousin Susan, all arrive together in a car from New York, with bags of deli food from Zabar's. There are loud happy greetings when they see Sarah, a flurry of embracing and kissing and chatter—*Did you have a good summer, sweetheart?* Nana asks her, *Have you enjoyed the house? I'll be back next week, when are you going home?* and Sarah nods, smiles, excuses herself to clean up the kitchen—punctuated by Emily's groans and Michael's frustrated efforts to hook up the water hose to the birthing tub properly, and the oven timer *dinging* on another done batch of bread. The midwife shows up at dawn, yawning but perky, just as Emily is easing into the tub. Michael crawls in behind her, so she can lean against him. Sarah gives them both a mouthful of crushed ice. Rachel and Elijah lean over the tub, patting ripples into the water with their small, sticky hands. Nana, propped by her walker, and Leah, Sid, Rose, and Susan press near, their mouths all dropped into open, giddy smiles. Sarah remembers Emily's mother Leah making her all those snacks after school, the bananas with chunky peanut butter and homemade squash soups, with those same big, caretaking smiles on her face, and Emily's father Sid driving her home after it got dark, waiting to make sure there was someone there before driving off so Sarah wouldn't be all alone. *Okay, so you'll be okay, Sarah?* She remembers wanting to go back to Emily's house, just stay and live there all the time. Emily's family, robust, huge with cousins, grandparents, uncles and aunts, Emily's color-coordinated outfits, Leah playing board games with them, trying on makeup with them, buying Sarah her first box of Tampax, taping one of Sarah's drawings to their refrigerator, and Sid showing up at school events, even the daytime ones, the Open Houses, the art shows, cheering loudly for Sarah, too, because she was there alone, buying one of Sarah's girlhood paintings for twenty-five dollars to hang proudly on his office wall, dancing with Sarah at Emily's Bat Mitzvah and Sweet Sixteen parties, teaching Sarah how to ride a bicycle—*not* her father, she suddenly remembers, sees, it was *Emily's* father Sid who taught her, even that was Emily's, the father who ran alongside the wobbly, released-from-his-grip bike, applauding and cheering her on, the father who knelt and comforted her, cleaned her skinned knees, Emily sharing all that with her, but none of it ever really hers.

But the lemons in your hair, that was yours, she reminds herself, you had that. Your own mother combing your hair, and your own father at the beach, watching to make sure the waves didn't carry you off and disappear you forever. And the birthday parties, the real, once-upon-a-time parties, before her brother died, when it was still okay to celebrate that she was there and alive. She had that, it was real and they were there, they gave her all of that. Before they were broken or disappeared. They did their best.

So, that's it, then, why isn't that enough for you, it has to be. Lemons and ocean waves and candles on cakes. A mouthful of honey. Your parents, waving to you from shore.

The labor gets worse, and the groans more ragged, and a thrill flares through Sarah, a delight in every looming, ugly, torturing second of it. When Emily starts to scream from somewhere deep inside, Sarah gulps from her glass of McCallan and thinks about hospitals and doctors, and what if something's really wrong this time, maybe she needs an episiotomy or a Cesarean. Maybe they should just hack her open like a chicken. Or they could go at Emily's belly like it's a piñata, the whole family taking turns with a broomstick. She wonders if having this baby's going to kill Emily, tear her up for real, spill all her insides so the tub is a giant vat of drained-out, frothy Emily-blood, and a dead Emily, Michael crying, everyone hysterical at losing her, the baby still lodged inside, gotten rid of with Emily, and then they'd all turn to her, Sarah, she'd be all they had left, their child, wife, mommy, and they'd all put their arms around her and let her hold back on. It would all be hers, the house in the country with the sheep and the ducklings, the garden and buzzing, endlessly honey-rich bees, the nanny to raise the kids, the maid to clean, the rich husband, the healthy, able mother and father there to take care of her and keep her safe, the art on an easel just waiting for when she felt like getting around to it, because it doesn't matter, there's plenty of time, no *tick tick tick*, there's nothing at stake, nothing to prove or define. Even the tub full of hot blood would be hers, if she wanted to bathe in it like the Countess in the painting and be frozen in young time forever, all of this would be her home, hers.

Emily screams, and Sarah stumbles over it, blinking, then steps back behind everyone to get out of the way, retreats to the kitchen, gets a handful of ice from the freezer, and there, taped to the refrigerator, is her little-girl crayon drawing: colorful flowers, a happy sun beaming spokes of sunshine, a doggy, three sheep, ducklings, *My Family*, two grown-up and two child-sized smiley stick figures all holding hands before a thatched-roof cottage. My perfect happy family.

No, it isn't hers. It's Rachel's drawing, she realizes. It's not her family, her house, it never will be. It's all a mere fantasy, a birthday candle wish. A childish game of pretend.

She pours more whiskey.

Emily screams again, and, leaning sideways from the edge of the room, Sarah can still see into the tub; she can see the flush of cloudy liquid from between Emily's legs, displacing the tub water with its thrust, first white, then a brilliant crimson, then the dark crowning of Ariel's head. Emily takes a slow, deep moan of breath as Michael presses his mouth to the side of her damp forehead. The midwife slides her fingertips just enough inside Emily to coax out a thin lump of shoulder, then, in another brief bright swirl of blood, a white glow of skin, the baby comes rushing through, kicks its legs free of its folded, packed-tight shape, and opens its tiny tadpole underwater mouth. The midwife lifts the dripping body from the water and settles it onto Emily's heaving chest. Leah and Sid hug each other, Nana is clapping her hands with joy at the birth of her seventh great-grandchild, Rachel is squealing, wanting to touch the baby, and everyone else slowly begins to breathe just as the baby takes its first whimpering choke of air. The dun-colored cord still links from the baby's belly down into the water, into Emily, and from where Sarah is standing the refraction at the water's surface gives the illusion that the cord has already been sliced in two.

FALL

SHE AWAKENS TO the sound she's grown used to: crickets, grasshoppers, and cicadas, swarming bees, their relentless insect rasp. But the clear white light through the windows is seashore light, greenless and blank, and she remembers, after a moment, that she's back in Rockaway.

The buzz of wings in her ears transmutes to crashing waves, and instead of diapers and fruit and oatmeal she smells turpentine, linseed oil, the meager blots of paint on her palettes. And curry, left in the air from Avery's dinner the night before, the scent that had greeted her as she walked into the kitchen, hot, tired, yoked with her suitcase and bags of fading vegetables.

"Ah, you are home now! And Emily is having her baby?" He'd beamed, as if beside himself to see her back, and heaped her a plate of basmati rice. She realized that with Bernadette in Sri Lanka the empty house must have seemed very lonely, and so she ate her dinner in the kitchen with him, just to be polite. They sat facing each other and sweating at the rusting, unstable TV tables he and Bernadette always ate on. She showed him the zucchini and tomatoes and basil she brought from Connecticut, and over their curry he boomed for her a long speech on Sri Lankan produce. She finally interrupted to ask if anyone had called while she was gone, if there were any messages. Only her parents, he told her. They were missing her, looking for her, sounding worried, why was she not answering her cell? No, no, there is no emergency, but they called many times; they will call again tomorrow. She must be missing them, too, he stated loudly, When is she going home, Why did she not tell them she was going to Emily's, She must call them, She must let them know she is fine, When is she going home? All proclaimed in his thundering voice, yelling rebuke at her, chastising her stubborn, pointless flight, her hideous self-indulgent selfishness, and she winced over her plate. Then she remembered how he and Bernadette used to yell at each other, blasting the house with their lilts, how she used to cringe, sitting on her bed and eating her dinner in her room upstairs, at the harsh familiar clap of their words until the day she realized, spotting the beige plastic snailed in each of their ears, they were both just hard of hearing.

She promised Avery in a modified return yell that she'd call her parents first thing in the morning. He nodded, satisfied. What an idiot she was, to think Marty might have called, looking for her. Wondering when she was coming back. She hadn't called him from Connecticut. Let *him* wait for the phone to ring, she'd thought. Let him wonder about *her*, what she was doing, what kind of small or large gap his absence might be creating in her carefully occupied-elsewhere day. Let him wonder if the lack of him digs in sharp, if it leaves a print. Or if it's just rinsed away, like a footshape in sand swirls off to grainy water beneath a wave.

It's Friday night, she thought, watching Avery chew. He must be at Itzak's for shabbes dinner. Practically down the street. She pictured the family singing like some flame-of-God, End of Days church choir, Itzak pouring her a fat snifter of brandy, Marty nudging over his prayer book so she could see, under the table placing her hand on his thigh.

She didn't bother to ask Avery if anyone else called. Instead, she inquired if he'd heard from Bernadette, how she was doing.

"Yes, she is calling me from home every Sunday. The surgery for cataracts is very successful. I am very relieved."

I think I left something to drink in the fridge, she thought to herself, and squeezed herself up to look. Two Heinekens, good. German beer, my shabbes Kiddush. The thought amused her. Should dig up some storm or birthday candles around here, recite the blessing. Avery'd get a kick out of that. She chuckled to herself.

"She is staying now with our oldest daughter Celeste, in Colombo. Our home used to be there, before we are coming here to New York. But when we married, we lived first in Trincomalee. Also by the sea. Always, we are living by the sea."

"That's nice."

"Here, I will show you . . . " He got up eagerly, his swollen knees almost tipping the TV table, and disappeared to rummage through boxes in the storeroom off the kitchen.

"Oh, no, don't bother," Sarah called. She hadn't a clue where Sri Lanka was, didn't really care. "That's okay," she called again, pouring her beer into a glass. She expected an atlas or a globe, a travelogue of every single, poignant place by the sea he and Bernadette ever lived. Her mouth burned from the curry, and she hurried to swallow half the glass of beer before he came back.

He returned with a flowered, gold-ringed photo album, moved her food aside, and propped it open at the first page. A sepia-toned wedding photo of Avery and Bernadette clutching hands, younger by forty years, with thick hair and full-toothed smiles, their stretched lips a brownish black, his military uniform bland as mushroom, her satin gown a dull spread of milk.

"Nice," she said lamely. "You both look really happy." She wondered if they'd shouted their vows at each other. She finished the beer and opened the second bottle.

"And here, we are on our honeymoon in Bombay. Here is our first child, Peter, with Bernadette in the hospital. And here is our daughter Celeste, and here is Bernadette after giving birth to our younger son Kirin, and here are Celeste and Nissa at school . . . Nissa, she is now a doctor!" The cellophane crackled up, peeling back from the smiling photos like a layer of dead skin, and he carefully smoothed each page down as he went.

"Yeah," she said, sipping her beer. "Bernadette told me. It's wonderful."

He passed through the beaming births, parties, and school graduations of five children and seven grandchildren. By Kirin's third birthday the photos turned to Kodachrome, the children's cadmium yellow plastic toys, school uniforms in barite greens and aniline blues, the girls' lipsticks red as alizarin beets. All primary hues, lurid as parrots. The photos reminded her of the book of shells upstairs, and her own little half-painted shell, all those vivid, glossy color plates putting her attempt at a shell to shame.

A photograph is a dead image, a painting gives life! Not always, she thought. Not necessarily.

"Peter and Kirin are living here now with their families in New Jersey. We are hoping to bring Celeste and her sisters soon, with their families. They are grown-up women now, of course, but it would be good, we would like to have them here."

"That's nice," Sarah said again. She gingerly poked the album aside, so she could get back to her food. "Could we . . . ?"

"Oh, I am sorry. Excuse me." Avery closed the album, and wedged it between his thick thigh and the arm of the chair.

"So, when is Bernadette coming home?"

"Very soon. I am hoping to have her back soon, we must ready the house."

"For what?"

"For winter. We must take the screens down. I must check the shutters and the storm windows. It is getting very cold here, during the winter months."

"Sort of hard to imagine that." She waved her hand in front of her face to indicate heat.

"Ah, this is too spicy for you, this food?" he inquired.

"No no, it's great."

"It is hot now, but then unexpectedly will be very cold. Bernadette helps me with the house every year, now. I am too old to do this all alone."

"Oh, you're not old, Avery." She guessed he wanted her to say that.

"I am sixty-four!" he announced. "Bernadette and I are married forty-two years."

"Congratulations." She toasted him with the last of her beer. She got up, looked again in the refrigerator, although she knew it was no use.

"Tell me, you are seeing Pearl at Emily's? Her hip is better now?" he asked. Yes, she told him, Nana's hip is good, much better. And yes, Nana will be coming home next week. Very soon. Just a few days. Coming back to Rockaway, back to her own house. Sarah looked over Avery's bald head, at the calendar hanging on the kitchen wall, a giveaway from the pharmacy on 116th Street. It still showed August—a picture of a robust, cheery octogenarian in a deck chair, holding a kitten and a bottle of Centrum Silver—but no, Sarah remembered, it was actually September. September 5th. Almost fall.

"Well, that is good, Pearl coming home. I am missing her."

"Yeah, Nana's great."

"A wonderful woman."

"She's so sweet, letting me stay here all this time."

"And her return is good for you as well, then! You will be going home, too!" he declared. "You must miss your own home, with your family. Eat more, the spicy food is good in this heat."

He reached to spoon out more curry, but she got up again, hastily, almost knocking over the rickety little table, and told him she was full, thanks, the trip back from Connecticut was really tiring, a train, a subway, a bus, all just to get home, or get here, a long day, sorry, she really just needed to go to bed. Looking in cabinets as she said it, searching, *There's* something, she thought, thank God. She said good night to Avery; he shrugged, and pleasantly, silently nodded good night. She dropped her beer bottles in the trashcan, stood awkwardly until he moved his dishes to the sink, his back to her, then, reaching into the cabinet, grabbed the dusty, unopened bottle of cooking sherry. As she left, suitcase in one hand, sherry in the other, she saw Avery lean to reach into the trashcan; he removed her bottles and dropped them into the glass-recycling bag with a dull double-clink. She saw him retrieve out the photo album, and open it again on the empty TV table. He started right back at the beginning wedding photo, turning and smoothing the pages very slowly. The cellophane crackled after her up the stairs.

———

STILL IN HER sleep T-shirt, she makes herself coffee with the last of an expensive bag of beans. She counts them out into the grinder. Twenty-nine beans. She can't believe it takes twenty-nine beans just to make one cup of coffee. It seems excessive, wasteful. She finds rye bread dusted with hoarfrost in the freezer, but there is no milk. The butter she'd left in its dish on the counter has gone rancid in the heat. She will have to go shopping, ride the pink bicycle into town. Maybe stop at the bakery for a fresh seeded rye. Or a challah. No, wait, it's Saturday, they'll be closed. Should've brought a loaf of zucchini bread back from Emily's. The thought of going anywhere, doing anything, of pedaling thirty torrid blocks just to buy food, exhausts her. And what's the point, you're leaving soon, why spend the money, why bother stocking up on food? She inspects the refrigerator again, wishing she'd saved one of the Heinekens. She breaks off a slice of frozen rye bread and gnaws at it, presses it against her overhot cheek.

The house is very still. Avery, he's working at the dime store, she thinks. She looks out the kitchen window, toward the ocean, sipping her coffee. Bitter. Probably that weird tap water here, all those minerals, God knows what's in it. She brushes a caraway seed from her chin. Maybe go for a long walk if it cools off later, if the beach isn't too crowded. Maybe even go swimming, if the jellyfish aren't bad. You can't leave here without even once going in the ocean, how crazy would that be? What a waste. Nana's coming back soon, you'll have to leave soon. Go home. Go somewhere. *Tick tick tick.* It's so hot, the air so airless and flat. Why didn't Avery ever install a ceiling fan in here? She could call Emily, see how they're all getting along. How the baby's doing. If they've planned for his Bar Mitzvah yet, if they've started his college fund. She could unpack, do laundry. Then start repacking. She spots the wall calendar again, August still hanging. She tears off the old month, crumples up the page, and tosses it in the bag of paper recycling. There, September, 2001. A photo of a trim, business-suited mother doling out One-A-Day Vitamins to her orange-juice-sipping children. You have been here almost four months. The clamshell she found on the beach her first day is still on the kitchen sink, now cradling a dirty-looking, flesh-colored sponge.

She returns to her room with her coffee, brims the cup full from the bottle of cooking sherry. She changes into shorts and a bikini top. She brushes sandy grit from her feet—I've always been so careful, she thinks, how does all this sand still get in here?—puts on a pair of sandals. Not too many days left, for walking on the beach, for swimming. You should do that, take full advantage of your last days here. You should call your parents so they know you're alive, so they're not hysterical. You should call the gallery woman, give her an update. Tell her how well things are coming together. How focused and expressive and defined you and your work are, now. How interesting. Maybe ask for more time. Maybe she'll give you more time.

She gathers and stuffs a load of berry-stained clothing into Nana's relic of a washing machine. Why bother doing laundry, she thinks, you're leaving soon, Nana's coming back in a few days, she'll want her house back, she'll kick you out. You'll have to go, have to go somewhere.

She sips her coffee-sherry, washes the Connecticut vegetables in the cloudy, lukewarm kitchen faucet water, contemplates making bruschetta. Shouldn't waste all that fresh basil. Can't blame Nana, it's her house. You should call United, schedule a flight home. Why didn't you do that earlier, it's going to cost a fortune to book a flight this late, and you're almost out of money, anyway. Your parents'll be so happy, you'll stay with them, of course. There's nowhere else to go. Just for a little while. Then you'll get your things out of storage, get a new place to live, get a new job. Start over, all over.

She leans against the kitchen counter, feeling breathless. You can balance their checkbook, change the smoke detectors, all watch TV together. Make up for lost quality time. The least you can do for them. Make them happy. She pictures them at the dining room table, the three of them, eating a heart-friendly casserole. Many, many casseroles. She will cook them casseroles every night, night after night. She will live in her old room, her little-girl room, sleep in her girlish twin bed. You should start packing everything up. All your things, get all those blank canvases to UPS, the unused tubes of paint, send it all home. She hears the house phone ring—There they are, waiting for me, she thinks, they are sitting there hungry and nervous and waiting, I'll call them later, later, there's still time—and hurries outside.

It's already searingly, blindingly, headache-inducing bright; families in bathing suits are already trudging past the house with coolers and folded lounge chairs, noses creamed white with zinc oxide, heading for the beach. Kids clutching plastic buckets and shovels, dragging their garish beach towels in the road. September, fall is coming, is here, enjoy what's left of your summer, kids. She wonders if they would let her build a sand castle with them, collect whatever broken shells are left.

Down at the intersection of her street with the boulevard she sees other families walking on their way to the synagogue at 135th Street, the men in their heavy black suits, the women wearing flowered pastel dresses, nylons and pumps, and summer straw hats. Strolling on shabbes. How can they dress up like that in this heat? she muses. Nylons, probably wearing slips, too, under those long dresses, oh God. She tries to imagine the life of these people living here forever, trapped in Rockaway, for twenty-five years in a creaky, warping house on the beach, the consuming roots of it, the loud neighbors, the deadening fray of children, hurrying for challah on Fridays and steaming in synagogue on Saturdays, the boggy sponge of time rising up slowly, slowly over their heads. Like quicksand. Like compost. She wonders why they aren't all gasping for air.

She wishes she were still in Connecticut, tweezing ticks off the dog, knitting baby-sized thousand-dollar sweaters, making a lifetime of pesto for Emily's family, an outline of her life traced onto theirs and leaving her to live in all that clean, empty space in the middle.

She wishes she were in Russia, France, Spain, wandering around and studying other dead people's garishly framed paintings, sweating in sex with revolving, negligible men, all of her lightweight unrooted life packed neatly, disposably, maplessly, in one tote bag, one nylon knapsack.

She wishes she were in Cuba with Julius, sipping a seventeen-dollar banana daiquiri at Hemingway's favorite Havana bar. She'd be sweet and fresh as mint, wearing an oyster-colored linen dress, sipping her drink, cool and dewy, Julius whipping out a credit card, ordering cracked crab on ice, more drinks, everything done and decided for her, the whole world focused down to that sustained moment, and she could live there, in that endless moment, forever.

Maybe maybe that little-girl bed, yes, maybe she can crawl back between those smooth blank sheets, back under the coverlet and stay there, go back to sleep, go back. What did that coverlet look like? She tries to remember the bedspread, the one she slept under all those childhood years, ate all those paper-plate dinners on top of, but suddenly can't. Was it flowered, embroidered, eyelet? She can't even remember the color, but it's there, waiting for her, it must be. She can't remember the smell of the room: plastic purses and jewelry, licorice candy, fruity adolescent make-up, waxy crayons, acrylic paints? She can't summon up any of it, as if it's been erased, scraped from her mind with a palette knife, scumbled over with a thick layer of titanium lead white. She wishes she could vanish entirely now, too, like in a cartoon where the disappearing thing takes its black hole with it.

A kid zooms past her on a beribboned Schwinn—Hey, watch out, lady!—startling her up onto the curb. She peers down the street one last time, looking. She goes back into the house.

⁓

"GOOD MORNING, Medical Office."

"Hi, it's Sarah Rosenfeld? I'm a patient of Dr. Brandon's? I wanted to leave a message for her?"

"Oh hi, Sarah. Hold on a sec, she's in today, I can get her for you . . . "

"Oh, okay. Thanks." Sarah waits. It's even hotter upstairs, here in her room. She takes a warm sticky swig from the sherry bottle, looks out the huge picture windows, at the florid color plates she ripped from her shell book and scotch-taped over the faces of Nana's family, at the shells still laid out on the dresser like flatware, at her wood case of fat paint tubes, her abandoned canvases and color-gobbed palette. Her palette knife. Her one begun painting, ivory and iron oxide black, still propped up on the easel, waiting.

These are timid choices, Sarah, her professor had said. *Barely choices at all . . .*

"Hello, Sarah?"

"Hi, yeah, Dr. Brandon. I didn't think you'd be there."

"I've got office hours on Saturday mornings now."

"Oh, that's terrible," Sarah says. "You shouldn't work on Saturday."

"Just until noon. Everything okay?"

The smell of her oil paints is getting to her. Queasy stomach. Dull pain at the back of her head, just inside her skull, tapping to get out. She gulps sherry.

"Sarah?"

"Oh, yes, I'm fine, it's just, I'm out of town, I'm away on sort of a retreat, you know, I'm a painter and . . . " She tries to steady her voice, stay focused, " . . . and anyway, I brought four months of Ortho-Novum with me, because that's how long I thought I'd be away working here, getting ready for this big exhibit? But I'm thinking about staying away longer? Not coming home yet? I'm just thinking maybe. I'm just trying to figure out my plans."

"No problem, I'll put Bonnie back on, just give her the number of a pharmacy wherever you are, she'll call it in."

"Okay. Uh . . . "

"Anything else?" Dr. Brandon sounds pleasant, as always, preoccupied, unconcerned.

"Yeah, I just . . . " She swallows again from the sherry bottle, sets it carefully on the floor. "Well, we talked once about if I ever wanted to have kids, remember? And I said no, I didn't, but you said if I ever did it wouldn't be any problem for me? Remember?" She wanders closer to her easel, stumbles, grips the wooden frame. She tries to steady herself.

"That was a while back, but . . . " Sarah hears papers shuffling. "Hey, did you get married, Sarah?"

She thinks she hears Dr. Brandon smile, happiness for her in her voice. "Oh, no, nothing like that," she says, quickly. "I'm not getting married, or anything." She makes *ha ha* noises into the phone. "I've just been thinking. You know, you have a kid, that's really what your whole life becomes all about. Feeding the baby, taking care of the baby. Being totally focused for years and years on this other little person you've created. Serious, important cycle-of-life stuff, right?"

"Sure, yeah. Well, let's see, you're how old now?"

"Almost thirty-five."

"Well, let's not worry yet. Just go off the Ortho-Novum and try for a few months. Let's see what happens."

"Well, no, I don't want to *try*." She leans, peers at her canvas, her little shell.

"You don't?"

"I just want to know what my options are. *If* it's an option, still. Like, yes or no. So I know."

"I can't really tell you that, at this point."

"Yeah, but that's what I'm trying to figure out. If I just waited and stalled and did nothing for too long, and now it's too late ... "

You're too frightened of color. You're too dependent on a monochromatic palette.

" ... and now it's all over and decided for me. If it's that black and white."

You think it's safe, staying there, don't you? You think it's bold.

"Or if, you know, if I still get to choose my colors."

"What do you mean?"

"Like crayons in the box, remember that? When you were a kid?"

"Oh, right."

"You'd open the box and all that color's waiting for you. It's like a thousand pointy little rainbows in there. You know you can draw anything. You can draw the whole world. You want to grab every one of them and start scribbling." She laughs again, a little. "I probably sound so *painterly*, right? So, whoa, crazy artist, here!" She feels dizzy, closes her eyes, tries to breathe deep. "I'm sorry, Dr. Brandon, what did you say?"

"I said, why don't you come see me when you're back in town? We can run some tests."

"Tests?"

"But it's too soon to worry about anything. So, don't worry. Okay?"

"I'm not *worried*," she says. Of course, she thinks, this woman is a scientist, not an artist, how can she possibly understand? She's been feeling my ovaries, groping my insides, for fifteen years, and thinks she knows me, thinks that's an answer. Don't worry. Sure, just don't worry . . .

"Sarah?" She hears impatience in Dr. Brandon's voice. You shouldn't be bothering her, she has important scientist things to do.

"Yeah, okay." She reaches, touches her abandoned palette. The blots of dried color feel like plastic. Aureolin yellow, rose dore madder, dioxazine purple, viridian, pthalo blue, all a waste. "Whatever. I'll just call you when I get home. Thanks, really. Bye." She hangs up. She is so thirsty, thick-tongued, where did she leave the sherry bottle? So expensive, these paints. Old Holland Series VI, a hundred and sixty-five dollars a tube. When she bought them for herself she'd pictured old men grinding away at the madder by hand, dribbling in the linseed oil on a marble porphyry table, painstakingly filling the tubes just for her, for all her important work. She'd thought it was worth it at the time. Their purity, their intensity is what makes them valuable, gives them such strength. Those thick tubes in her wooden case could've gone far, lived a long, long time. Created so much. She feels pain at wasting them; she feels guilt that she left them all to linger in this heat and dry up and die. She closes her eyes, feels her professor wrench the brush from her hand,

I don't care if it works or not, if it clashes. Get your hands dirty, Sarah. Mess it up. That's what's bold.

She sees him violently squeezing tubes, smearing her canvas,

Otherwise you'll never have any depth. You'll have no true perspective. No harmony. You'll have nowhere to go.

She hears her phone ring. Twice, three times. She needs a drink, needs to drink some water. That's what you need, a glass of fizzy, cloudy water. She realizes she has clenched her fists, feels her fingernails digging in her palms, makes herself stop. She flexes her sweaty hands. She feels the sour heat of a headache. It's fall, summer is over, why is it still so hot? She feels her blood is bubbling, in a simmer. Her mouth is dry. She opens her eyes, sees the bottle of sherry on the floor, grabs, takes a final swig. The last drops are horribly warm and syrup-sweet in her mouth. She needs some water.

The phone rings again, the house phone this time. She wishes it would stop.

She picks up her palette knife, crusted with dead red paint. Crimson, scarlet, burgundy, cerise. She grips the smooth wooden handle. She touches, presses the blade to the tips of her fingers, a dull blade, not meant to cut, but its edge is steadying. She presses harder and looks at her painting on its easel, the insignificant little shell. Nothing but some charcoal scratches, a few sad ivory and bone black dabs. No harmony, no depth. She scrapes the corner of the knife along her inner arm, where the skin is so pliant, so fragile and thin. She admires the faint white skin-scrapes, like foreign-language letters, faded skywriting, cuneiform, hieroglyphics on papyrus. An indecipherable message, a hidden wisdom. She pushes the tip against her wrist, senses the pulse there, ticking. She angles the blade, scrapes the full length of her arm, stretching skin. She'd stretched all her canvases so carefully before leaving for Rockaway, scraping her elbows and knees by crawling around the harsh cloth on all fours, using the frame and stretcher she'd built herself to make all those perfect, hopeful, stretched-taut squares. She glances at all those canvases, pushed into a stack in the corner of the room. Their backs are to her, now, rejecting her. Only the one canvas on her easel, her one painting. Insignificant little empty shell.

But there was never any hope for this painting, she realizes, not from the exact second she started it. It's a *blank* canvas that's full of promise. An unstained, unscarred canvas hasn't been attempted and ruined and failed at yet. The insult, the sin, is what she has both done and hasn't done to this canvas, and it is too late to start over, time is up, it's all over, too late.

She regrips the knife, makes a lunging slash at the canvas; it shudders on its easel, but there's no rip, no tear. She grabs the frame in her other hand to steady it, tries a stab, and this time she stabs through, punctures the canvas so hard her hand slams deep, bruisingly, against her shell; she drops the knife and uses her fingers and hands to rip more, rip harder and wide, skinning her knuckles and tearing the canvas into shreds.

She is panting for breath. But still the simmer, the boil.

She gathers up the tubes of paint, clutching them to her chest like tiny nursing rodents, and hurries downstairs to the kitchen, dumps them on the counter. She kicks the main trashcan out from behind the door. She unscrews a tube of alizarin crimson and squeezes, gasps, no matter how accurately the tubes are color-labeled, so you think you know exactly the shade, the tint, the value you're getting, there's always a shock when you see it, see the richness of it. A good shock. Like the difference between blood sealed inside the branching blue lines on your wrist, your thighs, the tender inner flesh of your arms, and the abrupt vivid happy red of it when released.

The paint coils in thick strings into the trashcan. She touches a finger to it, swipes it across the back of her hand like a lipstick trial. She opens a tube of ultramarine blue, squeezes it all out carefully from the bottom, adds a smear of blue to her skin. Pretty. She releases a tube of cadmium yellow after it. Good. The primary colors, like a circus. She starts on the secondary colors, the tertiary colors, all the colors on the wheel. The color wheel, Ferris-wheel-spinning in her head. One by one she empties out tube after tube. The colors' moist coils weigh down the trashcan's plastic liner, settle into sedimentary layers. She looks, thrusts her hands in, breathing hard. A bold, clashing, dirty mess, yes.

SHE TRUDGES DOWN the brilliant white span of beach as far from the water and oily, screaming flock of beach-goers as she can get. The hot sand humps itself over and over in small mock dunes, and her sandaled feet sink into it, making the walk harder.

She feels thick-mouthed, plastered with heat. *There is nothing colder than the sun at its height in the summer*, Pissarro said that once, or Renoir, something about how hard it is to paint snow, that nature is colored in winter and cold in the summer. Whatever. I ought to have put sunscreen on, she thinks, but then remembers something she read once, that most skin damage occurs during childhood, anyway. That's when cancer starts. It just takes so long to grow, turn lethal. And by then it's too late.

A reclined and glistening group of cocoa-buttered, seal-brown teenage girls in string bikinis look oddly at her as she stumbles past, but she can't imagine why.

Marty's door is slightly ajar, the screen closed but not locked. She taps quietly, then again, louder.

"Hello?" she calls. "Hello?"

There's no answer, no sound from inside. She doesn't know what else to call. *It's Sarah* is too formal, *It's me* too assuming, presumptuous. Maybe he isn't even home, maybe he's out strolling. There's a pebble in her sandal. The walk here has left her sweaty; her face hurts from squinting out the sun, her skin is at blister range. She is so thirsty. She wants some water, clear icy water. No, she wants a crystal, silver-filigreed glass of iced vodka, yes, just touched sweet pink with apricot schnapps. How lovely that would be. She wants a bath of it to crawl into, to cool her and soothe. The inside hallway looks soft and dark. Past the hall, into the dining room, she sees the two lighted white candles on the table, left to burn down. She hears murmuring, more than one voice. She takes off her sandals and leaves them on the step, then opens the screen door and enters, closing it quietly behind her.

"Hello?"

She turns into the murky living room, toward the murmuring. A group stands in silhouette against the window. Her eyes adjust, and she makes out Marty, his height, his longish hair, dressed in an inky suit and black velvet, gold-threaded yarmulke shaped like a pillbox hat. He is standing with Itzak and six, seven, nine other men, a black-clothed

and bearded blur, their white tzitzit fringes hanging from under their coats like tampon strings. They hold books the size
of bricks, Hebrew letters spiking and cramming the pages
like nails stuffed in a box. A minyan, a quorum of men for
prayers. It looks like a meeting of Amish Elders, a council of
Puritan Magistrates assembled to try the town witch. They've
come to burn her, press her to death with stones, drown her
in a murky pond. Their bone black clothing absorbs all the
light in the room, and she feels unable to breathe.

"Excuse me," she says. "I'm sorry," she says, taking a
step back. She stumbles. Tries to balance.

Marty sees her and his face blinks in surprise. "Hi," he
says, slowly.

"Hi."

"Where did you come from?"

"I got back," she says.

"Wow," he says. "Are you all right?"

"I'm fine," she says. "I'm good. I'm great. I'm just
thirsty."

"What happened to you?" His eyes flicker over her, and
she looks down at her arms, her chest—she's mottled with
paint. Her arms, chest, shoulders. Still wet, oily. Her hands
are gloved with it.

"Nothing," she says. "Look." She holds her hands out to
him, as if supplicating. "I was painting. I finished painting.
I'm finished. See?"

"Good. That's good, but . . . " He looks confused, takes a step forward. "Are you sure?"

"Nothing. I just . . . had to get out of the house. Get away. Now that it's done. I wanted to celebrate."

"Hello, Sarah," Itzak says. He smiles at her, drifting his fingers through his beard. The other men nod, and several of them go back to praying. Their mumblings rise and fall, a minor key, she remembers that, Frankie trying to teach her about music and harmonics. How the notes relate to each other, complement each other, something like that.

"Hello," she says primly. She wishes Frankie were here instead, with Tony and Sammy. She misses their fun, the light of their Mafioso jostling. The coolness in the room raises gooseflesh on her painted arms, the backs of her thighs. She sees her nipples poking through her bikini top. She crosses her arms in front of her, feeling indecent. Immodest. *Tzenius*, she remembers. She should have covered up. She wishes she were coated in a thicker, more opaque layer, a carapace of paint. She digs her bare toes into the carpeting.

"How's your friend?" Marty asks.

"Fine. If I ever had a baby, I'd have it at home. I'm a total disciple now."

"She was the doula," he informs Itzak. "Her friend had a baby at home, with a midwife. Beautiful, huh?"

"Ah," says Itzak.

She watches Itzak's hand stroking his beard, finds it oddly sexual. She shifts her weight, looks back to Marty. "And we lit candles on Friday nights," Sarah tells him. "Emily taught me the prayers in Hebrew."

His face brightens in pleasure. "That's good."

"The blessing over candles and the blessing over wine." But it doesn't mean anything to me, she thinks, nothing at all.

"I'm glad." He nods happily at her. "See, that's good."

"It was really beautiful," she says, "the light, the prayers." Empty ritual, just dead words, rote words. *Phylum Molluska, Mytilus Edulis.*

"That's good for you," he says. "I think that's really good for you."

"Yes," she says.

"So, hey—" Marty begins.

"No, I know," she says. "I just wanted to say hi. I knew you couldn't call, so . . . I'll just see you—"

"No, wait a minute."

"I'll see you later sometime."

"No, come on. Don't leave."

And where are you going to put me? she wants to ask. Where is it you think I can go?

He separates fully from the group of praying men, approaching her. "Come on, come up here," he says, indicating she should go upstairs.

"All right," she says. "Bye," she says back to Itzak. She begins to climb.

"We hope to see you next Friday, Sarah," Itzak says. "We'll have you say the blessings."

"Oh," she says. "I don't know them very well."

"'Every act carried out in sanctity is a road to the heart of the world,'" he quotes to her.

"Oh. Okay."

"'God's radiance glows in all human beings,'" he continues. "'But it does not shine in its full brightness within them. Only between them.'"

She rubs at her arms, smearing, coating herself. "Of course."

"That's good," Marty says to Itzak. "I'll give her that to read."

"So, come Friday," Itzak says to her. "We'll have margaritas and argue Buber. You can bring fruit." He returns to the other men, still caressing his wisps of beard.

Marty follows her up the stairs. She expects to feel his hand on her back, as if he's worried she might fall. But he doesn't touch her at all.

"Are you mad at me?" she asks over her shoulder.

"No," he says. "Why would I be mad at you?" They arrive at his bedroom. "Just stay here," he says. "We're going to shul again, and then I'll come back."

"You'll come back?"

"Yeah, I'll come back. Don't touch anything. Maybe you should get some sleep, or something."

"So, I can stay here? That's okay?"

"Yeah. Just stay here." He motions *stay here* with his hands, and starts to leave.

"I really do get what Itzak said," she tells his back. "It's like music, right? Or color? It's the same thing, it's how the notes and colors connect with each other that makes them beautiful. You just have to get the combinations right. Find the harmony."

"Yeah," he says. He stops, looks back at her, pleased. "It's like that."

"And remember you and I talked once, about how every act should be done with the consciousness of God?" He nods, listening, pleased. This is awful, what she's doing, she knows. Using God like bait. "And you said yeah, if there even is a God. But that everything you do has to create that communion. Remember?" Something to hold him, make him want to hold her.

"Yeah, I remember," he says. "That was a good day."

"And I told you I thought the angels would bless you. And that made you happy. Remember?" A spiritual striptease, trying to lure with a flash of soul. She feels ashamed of herself. He smiles at her, but he still doesn't touch her.

"I really get all of that now."

"Maybe you should take a bath," he says.

She looks down at herself again, at all the colors. Well, no, she realizes. She's smeared herself to mud, really, the final, neutral gray of overmixed colors, valueless and turbid as dirt. "A bath?"

He enters his bathroom and turns on the bathtub's gold, fluted spigots. A cloud of water blasts out. "You need a bath. You need to clean up. Go on." He nods, smiles gently at her, again, and leaves.

⁓

SHE FINDS THE vodka in the freezer, among bags of frozen chopped spinach and green beans, a cardboard box of Arm & Hammer Baking Soda, and three packages of Tabatchnick Cabbage Soup. His kitchenware is split in two sections, labeled with masking tape: *fleischig* in cabinets and drawers on the left, *milchig* on the right. She selects a big milchig tumbler, and pours. She drinks the glass down halfway. Why bother with the schnapps, she thinks, it's so pretty this way, so clean and clear and cold. So pure. She pours again to the top, and replaces the vodka in the freezer. She leaves oily gray smudges.

Upstairs, she tips a glass bowl of scallop-shaped soaps into the filling tub. She adds the contents of a bottle or two of bath gel from the wire basket, and presses on the Jacuzzi

jets. The water churns madly. She takes off her clothes and
steps into the foaming tub; she sits down cross-legged in
the bubbles, drinking from her tumbler of vodka and rubbing at her arms. This won't do it, she thinks. I need turpentine, naphtha. She plucks a washcloth from a folded pile on
the tub's marble ledge and scrubs away at her gray-smeared
skin. She swallows more vodka. A pumice stone, something
to strip away a layer. She spots a loofah in the wire basket and scours her arms. Maybe if I soak longer. Maybe I
need something more. She swallows more vodka, gets out
of the tub and inspects the cabinet beneath the marble sink.
Isopropyl alcohol, hydrogen peroxide, a cylindrical can of
Ajax, good, maybe that will help. She dusts the bathwater
heavily with it, splatting the bubbles flat, and gets back in
to soak. Maybe if the water's hotter. She turns off the cold
spigot, lets the hot water flow. She imagines Marty coming
back from shul and finding her still in the tub, gleaming
and purified. The fumes from the blistering steam sting her
nose, but the icy vodka is so cool in her throat. She leans
back, closes her eyes, sips. Her *milchig* tumbler, milk, that's
how the vodka tastes, like cold cold milk on a hot summer day, drinking milk and being eight years old, being
breastless, clean-fleshed, with lemon-bright hair falling to
her knees. She imagines Marty coming home and finding
her like that, back at the beginning, getting in the tub with
her, bathing her. She sees them curled up together in his

creamy, black-veined marble tub, floating together in an albescent clamshell at the top of a cloudy, uncrashed wave. He straps them in so they'll be safe, he tells her, they're taking a whimsical Playland ride, a spinning Ferris wheel, Hold on, hold on, and she wants to reassure him, No, this is safe for real, being together, being here with you. She drinks more milk and raises her arms to take off Marty's black cap, and he lets her, tipping his head into her neck. The cap slides off to reveal a space of pure, fluid light, no skin, no skull, no hair. The entry to his soul, open and radiant and welcoming, tinted to pearl by angels, just for her. The light pours from him to cover them both, a liquid, beautiful light. It fills the clamshell with blessing, with warmth, lulls her to a shade of home.

———

"HEY," SHE DIMLY hears him say.

She rubs her eyes. It's evening air in the room, air that's been breathed in and exhaled, heated all day but just starting to cool. She's on the bed, sprawled out naked under the top sheet.

"What time is it?" she asks.

"I don't know. Maybe seven, eight. After shul we went back to Itzak's. We had Havdalah." He's still wearing his

velvet and gold pillbox yarmulke. The candles downstairs
must have burnt out by now, she thinks. She watches him
take off his suit jacket, unbuckle his belt.

"You said you'd come back," she says.

"I didn't know you'd still be here," he says.

"But you told me to stay here. You said I could stay."

"Yeah, but I didn't *know*."

"So, you stayed there in case I wasn't here?" This makes
no sense to her. He sits on the edge of the bed to take off his
black leather shoes. He smells like onion, like wax burnt off to
smoke, like other men in black suits. When I am fifty-four he
will be seventy-eight, she thinks, he will be decrepit, riddled
with disease, and I will have to devote myself to taking care of
him. She cannot decide if she feels panic at this, or relief.

"I was sleeping."

"Good."

"Do you want me to leave?"

"No. Hold on." He goes into his bathroom, and she hears
his footsteps stop. "What'd you do in here? What happened?"

"You told me to take a bath."

"Wow."

She hears the sink tap running, the toilet flush, the
gurgle of liquid deep in a throat. He reenters the bedroom
in a T-shirt and boxer shorts, and now a little black knit cap.
He gets under the sheet next to her, wafting mint and baby
powder, tugging at her arm. "Come here."

She rolls over obediently, tucks herself against him. He pulls her arm to lie across his chest like a rib. "Shabbes is over," she says.

"Yeah." He looks down at her; the skin of arm, her shoulders and chest is still flaked with stubborn gray paint, but raw-looking, inflamed. "What is this? What did you do to yourself?"

"I tried to get it all off," she says. "But I'm clean, really. Good as new. I swear." She presses against him, stretches up, whispers into his ear. "Do you want me to leave?"

"No." He holds her tighter, and she angles her head toward him. When he kisses her, his mouth is soft, too casual. She wishes he would grip her harder, try to draw something out of her. She wishes he felt more urgency, need. She reaches down between them, slides her hand into his boxer shorts, feels he is already hard, good, and she wants him harder, affected. She wants him stricken with her. His hand slides down over her hips, but before his fingers can reach her, she knows she's still dry, she scrambles on top of him, pushing him on his back. She draws his shorts down, and takes him in her mouth. The best smell of him is there, the savory ripe leather of him; she works her tongue over him, her fingers gripping him slickly at his base, trying to inhale, absorb, whatever she can. But his hands in her hair are keeping her just enough back, off of him. She wants to make him come this way. His hands are over her ears, but she hears his jolted breathing, good, she wants him to come in her mouth, she'll draw him in that way, swallow all the light.

But he doesn't want that, she feels him pull away from her mouth. Her throat closes up without him there, and she wants to cry. He moves her gently onto her back; she just misses getting a clutch of his shirt as he sits up, rises from the bed.

"Wait a minute," he says. "I gotta get something."

"No, that's okay."

"What do you mean?"

"I mean, no, it's really okay," she says. "It doesn't matter. Just come back."

"What do you mean, it doesn't matter?"

She can't possibly explain to him why it doesn't matter. She shakes her head.

"Just hold on," he says, walking to the bathroom.

"Fine, okay. Whatever."

He comes back, rolling on a condom. He climbs on top of her, prodding her legs open with his knees. She knows she's still dry, that his entering her will hurt, draw blood, but she wants that, suddenly, wants to feel pierced, opened up, made raw. She winces at the first drive of his hips, at the rasp, and reaches down to touch the thin rubber lip of the condom as it sinks flush against her. She holds him there a moment, inside, but he draws back a sudden, abrading inch or two. It feels he's taking her skin with him. He pushes in again, and it eases. He pushes in, and the piercing goes sweet. He kisses her, and she sees them creeping forward together in the dark and he is holding a white candle out before them to shed light. Each thrust, each step, casts the light deeper into the darkness, illuminating it, brings the light deeper inside of her, and she wants it deeper inside of her, she wraps her legs around him to help, get it deeper, the light thrust fully inside. She moves her hips harder, wanting that burst between them, and feels a slip, something loosen. She tightens herself around him, squeezing.

"Hold on a minute," he says. He closes his face up tight, turns away from her.

"What?"

"Just . . . wait," he says. His breathing comes hard, then slows. The loosening expands, and her insides sag as she feels him slip out of her. "Man," he says.

"What happened?" she asks. "What did I do?"

"I don't know." He raises himself on an elbow, gropes between them a moment. "Lemme get this thing off." She hears the snap of rubber, and he flings the condom off the side of the bed. "I don't know," he repeats. He drops down on top of her again, his face still turned away.

"I'm sorry," she says. She reaches for him. "Maybe—"

"No, don't do that," he says, pushing her hand away.

She feels found out. She feels like treyf, like unholy meat. Like a leprous soul. No, she realizes. She doesn't have a soul. Because if she did have a soul, she would be precious to him. She would be a blessing, a thing to treasure and keep safe forever. He would open to her and shower her with light. But he's looked into her, and seen nothing, and now he knows and now she knows, understands at last. She's just been a body. A shell on the beach, a pile of compost. An illusion of depth. A plastic mermaid, left hanging on the rim of a dirty glass. No, falling, falling to the floor. No wonder she can't hold on to anything, her plastic arms have been snapped off and she is a cheap fake thing, emptied out and wholly without grace.

She waits until she hears him breathe in sleep, then gets up, gets dressed, and leaves.

THERE'S A MOON. There's a jumble of footprints. There are Drumstick and Baby Ruth wrappers, abandoned Fudgsicle sticks, a squeezed-out tube of Bain de Soleil. Crushed paper cups, their seams stained dark. Cigarette butts, sunflower seed shells, a broken plastic shovel, a tight ball of aluminum foil, a gnawed apple core. A pair of sunglasses missing one lens, an RC cola can, bent at the waist. Everything achromatic, a range of grays. The beach was so clean when she first arrived. She remembers her ritual of walking here, the breadth of warm, slipping sand, the tougher strip stiff with drying seawater, the wettest sand licked over and over by waves. Only seaweed and driftwood and feathers and shells when she arrived, and the endless hopeful sand. Now there's the messy trash of it, and the dead strewn jellyfish, and there's her. She remembers thinking the ocean looked different here, richer. Promising. She remembers wondering if women's cut-up bodies ever washed ashore here, how you know when that begins.

She hasn't been out here at night before. She's seen it behind glass, framed from her bedroom, the glints of wrinkling dark water, a ship's lights through fog. But she's in it, now, part of its depthless, toneless scheme. There's the flat white moon and the flat blacks of crumpled trash and the flat gray canvas of sand freckled with broken shells. She sweeps her hand through the dry sand, tries to draw a clean line, but the sand falls in upon itself, obscures her finger-traces among the labyrinth of foot tracks to multiple nowheres. There's a house alight with music and God to her left, and a house filled with photos of laughing, blood-linked people to her right, a house bursting with greens behind her in Connecticut, and far away west there's a house full of what's left of her own blood, facing another ocean, waiting for her. She tries to imagine another place, someplace left for her to go, but all she can picture is a 8' by 7' by 5' vault, a storage space she owns, temporarily, and only saw once, with wood-slatted sides and concrete floor, where everything left that belongs to her is boxed and blanketed away.

She looks across the moon-bright, swaying strip of wavecrash. She picks out of the mazed sand the singular footprint trail that leads to the sea. She gets to her feet and walks, and the prints fit her step by step, fit each step's heavy leaden weight until water touches her skin and the prints swirl away and she stops.

She pictures plunging in to the wet acid cold. She pictures the water sweeping her out, the firm sand dropping away beneath her. She feels herself letting go, how she might float off and disappear. The stinging jellyfish will burn her to ash, the sharks will shred her flesh, the tides will pull her close, drag her off in their angry embrace and she will let the deep water chill take her, choke off above her the last of air and color and light there is, that she'll ever have to see.

She takes another few steps and the black water teases, brushes against her ankles, her knees, and dances out again. She hesitates. She closes her eyes, smells sun-baked sand and towels, sweet fruit. She used to be able to do this, didn't she? Dive right in, blithe and carefree. The water is warmer now, and she leans, touches its softness, remembers frolic and splashing through waves. All by herself. Then a stumble, a crash, crashing and dizzy and getting back to her feet, looking toward land for assurance and applause and steadying foothold care to make sure everything was okay. To make sure she was safe in the world.

She turns, looks back toward shore. This time: no one, nothing is there.

She steps forward, deeper, the water rising to her thighs, her waist. A wave-ripple nudges her, lifting her up with gentle tease and catching her breath in her throat, then her feet touch sand again. But the water is insistent, pushing her about and off-balance. She turns her back to the next wave, digs her toes desperately for balance. She scans the deserted beach, the black blind shines of beach house windows, the vacant lifeguard chair. All of it, taunting her, daring her.

She hears a deepening hum, the sound of rising churn, feels the water abruptly pulling away from her, luring and stumbling her, and she turns, too late, to see a moon-glinting dark rise of water surging at and above her and too late to swim away or escape, and she is finally knocked fully off her feet by the crash, flipped and sucked under into the gritty salt cold.

The world blacks out and swirls, and she instinctively reminds herself not to breathe or swallow water. She feels her tumbling body intuitively unclench, uncompass itself, remember not to seek orientation. She feels her heart slowing down, her lungs pacing out the oxygen, her eyes recognizing the salt as ancestor. She feels her body relax and accept the roiling as truth. She feels herself lifted up again, the roil is sweeping her forward and her body is sailing, skimming, floating along toward shore, and she lets herself sail until she is lying victoriously safe, breathing hard and her cheek pressed against wet sand, the to-and-fro flirt of water still swirling her hair.

She remembers this. She scrambles up to her feet, remembers feeling this moment of alive and real and strong. I am here. That was the victory, she realizes. It was the emerging, the standing there on her own, panting and jelly legs and streaming salt foam, before ever looking for anyone or anything else to save her. It was her faith in the divine spark of her own life inside her little-girl belly and bones, the faith that allowed her to turn from the safe beach and race again and again back toward the chaotic, unpredictable waves. Because she will always reemerge. She will always get to her feet again, always be able to find her own way back to shore. Whatever awaits her or does not await her there. I am here, I am here.

She feels the shadows shifting, sees the sky brighten to a palette of rich pigments, coralline, ochre, aureolin, sees the gray sand around her warming to cream, the driftwood and jellyfish and shells and abandoned mess taking on definition and depth. She looks at the sea, now a rich, faceted green. Emerald, viridian, streaks of malachite. She sees all the clashing, harmonious colors of the world.

She drops to her knees, digs her hands into the sea-crisp sand. She traces a misshapen seahorse, a crooked mermaid. She scribbles them out with her fingers, levels the sand, draws them messily, imperfectly, again. She draws an entire school of joyous, unsymmetrical seahorses, a dancing gathering of clumsy mermaids. She draws a stick-figure little girl frolicking in the water, a mother and father waving from shore. She draws the swooping capital *M*s of flying seagulls. She draws a big childish sun sending out illuminating beams, draws the ocean's peaking, promising waves. She scrapes a castle into being.

ACKNOWLEDGMENTS

I AM SO GRATEFUL for the many forms of assistance I received for this manuscript—the close readings and wise editorial feedback, the supportive shoulders and endless patience during all those crazed phone calls. I'd especially like to thank Bernadette Murphy, Eloise Klein Healy, Emily Rapp, Tina Gauthier, Michelle Nordon, Askoid Melnyczuk, Cyndi Menegaz, Ellen Svaco, Mary Vincent, Rick Moody, Douglas Bauer, David Ryan, and Dylan Landis.

Boundless appreciation to my editor, Dan Smetanka, for his guidance, integrity, and impassioned faith, and to everyone at Counterpoint/Soft Skull Press. Enormous gratitude and respect to Michelle Henkin, and Mrs. Sylvia Perelson.

Please support the Rockaway Rescue Alliance and the Rockaway Waterfront Alliance, at: www.rwalliance.org.

© Michael Phillips

TARA ISON is the author of *A Child out of Alcatraz*, a Finalist for the *LA Times* Book Prize, and *The List*. Her short fiction and essays have been in *Tin House*, *The Kenyon Review*, *Nerve.com*, *Publishers Weekly*, and numerous anthologies.